**the stranger she was trusting to
treat her and her son right.**

A few minutes later the shower came on. She pictured him shampooing his hair, which curled down his neck a little, inviting fingers to twine in it gently.

Some time passed after the water was turned off. Was he shaving? Yes. She could hear the tap of his razor against the sink edge. If they were a couple, he would be coming to bed clean and smooth shaven…

Tonight she would sleep even better, knowing a strong man was next door. She could give up her fears for a while, get a solid night's sleep and face the new day not alone, not putting on a show of being okay and in control for Austin.

Now, if she could just do something about her suddenly-come-to-life libido.

THE COWBOY'S RETURN

BY
SUSAN CROSBY

Harlequin (UK) policy is to use papers that are natural, renewable, recyclable products and made from wood grown in sustainable forests. The logging and manufacturing processes conform to the legal environmental regulations of the country of origin.

Printed and bound in Spain
by Blackprint CPI, Barcelona

MILLS &
BOON

First published in Great Britain 2013
by Mills & Boon, an imprint of Harlequin (UK) Limited,
Eton House, 18-24 Paradise Road, Richmond, Surrey TW9 1SR

© Susan Bova Crosby 2013

ISBN: 978 0 263 90128 3
ebook ISBN: 978 1 472 00508 3

23-0713

Susan Crosby believes in the value of setting goals, but also in the magic of making wishes, which often do come true—as long as she works hard enough. Along life's journey she's done a lot of the usual things—married, had children, attended college a little later than the average co-ed and earned a BA in English. Then she dove off the deep end into a full-time writing career, a wish come true.

Susan enjoys writing about people who take a chance on love, sometimes against all odds. She loves warm, strong heroes and good-hearted, self-reliant heroines, and she will always believe in happily-ever-after.

More can be learned about her at www.susancrosby.com.

With gratitude to Kathy Coatney,
author and friend, who steered me
to some brilliant experts in their fields,
and who is a constant cheerleader.

And to Kirsten Olson,
a cheerleader for family-run orchards and farms.
Thank you for sharing your process and your passion.
Without your generosity, I could've gotten it all wrong!

Chapter One

Nostalgia struck Mitch Ryder with unexpected force as he drove the final miles toward home. He'd been out of the country and might have continued to stay away longer except his father had issued his fourth edict—more emphatic than previous ones—to get home or else. The Ryders were cattlemen, having ranched in this particular area of Northern California since the gold rush. Mitch was expected to pull his own weight in the family business, something he hadn't done for three years now.

As he drove, Mitch drew a deep breath, letting the heat of midsummer fill his lungs, savoring the magnificent view. The landscape changed with almost every mile—except for the spectacular sight of Gold Ridge Mountain, which was a constant, the centerpiece. The Red Valley surrounding it could be flat endless acres of hay or low grassy hills or orchards, all of it beautiful in its own way, but Gold Ridge Mountain dominated from every vantage point.

Nerves grabbed at Mitch as he neared the road leading to Ryder Ranch, gripped so hard he didn't make the turn but kept going. Twenty miles later, his gut finally unclenched, just before his truck coughed and lurched. "Are you trying to tell me something, Lulu?" he asked his prized old vehicle as she smoothed out. "I shouldn't have driven past the homestead?"

Mitch was only half kidding. He believed in omens. As a man who dealt with the realities every day of animals and often unforgiving land and weather, it probably seemed fanciful, but he'd learned to pay attention to his instincts, even if it was for something mechanical.

Like now. His truck coughed harder and lurched farther, signs of imminent death. He spotted the mailbox and private driveway of John "Barney" Barnard and turned in. Then Lulu died.

He checked his cell phone. No service.

Mitch didn't waste energy getting angry. He'd been asking a lot of the old girl to be in top shape after three years of neglect.

He started walking. The land looked different, less abundant, not the well-tended orchard it had always been. Barney's small, weathered house was blocked from view until Mitch got much closer, where the property looked better maintained, less of a jungle. Berry bushes stretched in orderly rows, and raised boxes held thriving plants, although the greenhouse was a dilapidated mess. Chickens pecked at the ground, ignoring him.

What had happened here? Barney had always been—
The front door opened, and out stepped a woman— maybe five-five, curvy, with long, blond hair pulled

into a ponytail. Younger than him, he figured, but not by much.

"It's about time," she said, plunking her fists on her hips. "Did you get lost? Or go on a binge?"

"Um, no, ma'am," Mitch said, entertained. He wondered who she'd mistaken him for.

"You were supposed to be here yesterday. That's what you promised on the phone. Look around. You can see how much work there is to be done."

Mitch swept his hat off and brushed it against his thigh as he considered her. She looked anxious, and sounded desperate.

"Well?" she asked. "Are you going to take the job? Room and board, just like we discussed, and a small salary. I can't do more than that."

His whole body relaxed as he settled his hat back on his head and moved a little nearer to the house. Mitch took her offer as an omen and went with it. She needed a handyman, apparently, and he'd just realized he could use a little adjustment time himself before going home. Whatever his father wanted was not something he was anxious to learn. "I keep my word, ma'am."

"Please don't call me ma'am. It makes me feel old."

He'd gotten close enough that he could see she had eyes the color of the moss that grew on rocks by the stream he'd played in as a boy, a dark, rich green with bits of gold—and annoyance—giving them some glitter. "What should I call you?"

"Annie. Annie Barnard." She stuck out her hand.

Mitch noted the dirt under her fingernails, the scrapes and scratches along her arms and hands. No wedding ring. He took a second, surreptitious, appreciative glimpse at her body. She would be a generous handful, that was for sure. He happened to like generous handfuls. A lot.

"Mom?"

"Come on out and meet... I'm sorry. I don't know your name."

"Mitch." He hesitated, waiting to see if she reacted to it. The Ryder family, generations of cattlemen, was well-known, but Mitch had been gone a long time, and this woman was a newcomer. When she didn't ask for his last name, he offered his hand to the boy standing beside her.

"This is Austin," she said. "He's ten. He's a great help."

The boy grinned, eyes the color of his mother's lighting up just like hers, his hair a shade darker blond and buzz-cut.

"Are you hungry?" Annie asked. "We were just sitting down to lunch."

"I could use a little something, thanks."

"Where's your gear?"

He hitched a thumb toward the road. "My truck broke down just as I arrived."

They entered the clean, cared-for house. Mitch hadn't been inside for years, but it looked pretty much the same as he remembered. Old, threadbare furnishings and rag rugs filled the space. Maybe the curtains were new. Framed photos scattered about were her own, but nothing else had her stamp on it.

"I'd like to wash up first," he said.

"Second door on the right."

He nodded his thanks and headed in that direction, wondering how any woman hired a guy off the street like that, without even knowing his full name, offering him a room in her house, trusting him around her son—and herself.

But then, he'd never been as desperate as she seemed to be. Maybe he would do all sorts of things not in the usual way if he found himself in the same straits.

He could give her a few days' help, give himself time to feel at home again. Win-win, he figured.

Annie Barnard let out a calming breath as she ladled chili into a bowl for the man, Mitch. No last name, apparently. It was fine with her. He'd come recommended, and they'd agreed she would pay him in cash anyway. What was one more risk?

"Did you run a background check on him, Mom?" Austin whispered.

Her ten-year-old knew way too much about the scary parts of life, Annie thought. "I'm a good judge of character, honey." The man spoke well, wore clean clothes, was freshly shaven. His dark brown hair had been professionally cut. And those brilliant blue eyes just plain ol' looked honest.

Most important, she needed help. Desperately. Right now. Even if it came from a one-named drifter with an unreliable truck and a strong, powerful body. He looked like he could manage the heavy lifting around her little farm.

Annie closed her eyes for a moment. She could not fail at this. She needed to be successful—for herself, but especially for Austin. He was entitled to a stable home and good role models, more than she'd ever had. She'd grown up in a family where people didn't live in houses long enough to establish a home or keep jobs long enough to become a career. She wanted roots for herself and her son. And she loved her ramshackle farm.

Mitch took a seat where she'd set the bowl. She passed him a basket with saltine crackers. The meal wasn't fancy, but it was filling. Soon they would have fresh vegetables from their garden. Almost everything she'd canned or frozen from last year's slim crop was gone. They ate a lot of protein-rich beans.

"This is great," Mitch said. "Good and spicy."

"Thanks. We have it a lot."

"A *whole* lot," Austin added. "Sometimes she mixes spaghetti into it. I like that."

"Sounds tasty," Mitch said. "What's first on your list of chores, Annie?"

"I bought a new high tunnel greenhouse, so the old one needs to be disposed of. We can pile it somewhere until we can get rid of it."

"All right. Mind if I push my truck closer to the house first? I'm hoping I can fix what's wrong with it myself."

"I've got a tractor you can use to pull it. You can put it in the shed, out of the weather, if you want."

"That'd be great, thanks," Mitch said. "How long have you owned this place?"

"My ex-husband inherited it from his uncle two years ago. We decided to give it a try. He didn't take to being a grower, but I did." The truth was she'd fallen in love with the farm and out of love with him. And he'd fallen out of love with both.

"I'm going to visit him in San Diego before school starts," Austin said. "My first airplane ride. You ever been on a plane, Mr. Mitch?"

"Just recently, in fact. I was working at a cattle ranch in Argentina. Do you know where that is?"

"No. Can we look it up on the internet?"

"We can do that."

"Was it fun?"

"Yes, and hard work."

"You can question Mitch after supper, Austin. For now we need to get to work."

That brought an end to the conversation. Soon after, they went outside. Annie drove the tractor as Mitch and Austin walked alongside.

"Wow! Cool truck!" Austin said, running to it. "I've never seen anything like that."

"Her name is Lulu and she's a 1954 Chevy," Mitch said. "She belonged to my grandfather. He gave her to me on my sixteenth birthday, so I've had her a long time."

"She looks good."

"I love this old girl. I've taken care of her." He ran a hand over her fender affectionately. "Unfortunately she's been sitting in someone's garage for three years while I was gone."

Annie wondered what that large, competent hand would feel like against her own skin. When she'd first spotted him from her kitchen window as he walked toward her house, she'd been worried. She couldn't see his face, just the cowboy hat, solid belt buckle, tight jeans and boots—the whole cowboy thing. She'd been ready to send him on his way. She needed help, but she didn't need anyone that good-looking, that tempting. Then he'd spoken respectfully and intelligently, including to Austin, and his appeal increased in a different way.

"Lulu's got five windows," Austin said as Mitch hooked up the tow chain from the tractor to the truck. "I've never seen that before. She kinda needs a paint job."

"Maybe someday I'll splurge for one. I'm fond of her flaws, though. I always think about my granddad when

I drive her. Annie, would you like to steer the tractor or the truck?"

"I'll take the truck. I've never pulled anything that big." She hopped inside the spotless vehicle, noted a large duffel bag on the floorboard. He'd been gone a long time. Were these his sole possessions?

Mitch came up to the driver's window. "Put 'er in Neutral, would you?"

"Does the seat move up? I can't reach the clutch."

He opened the door, found a lever and held it while she slid the whole split-bench seat forward. He smelled good. Clean. Not like aftershave, but like a breath of fresh air among the farm smells.

"Where's Neutral?" she asked, feeling ridiculous, but the gear knob wasn't etched with a diagram.

"Step on the clutch. Excuse me." He reached across her lap and wiggled the gearshift. "That's it. Just keep her true and steady. I'll do the work."

It took him a couple of seconds to take his arm away. Her thighs were on fire where he touched them. No man had laid a hand on her for a very long time. Now this sexy stranger was going to be living in her house, sleeping in the room next to hers, using the same bathroom.

He shut the truck door and jogged up to the tractor, where Austin was sitting, already forming an attachment to the man. "You allowed to drive?" Annie heard Mitch ask her son.

He shook his head. If Austin said anything, Annie couldn't hear it. It'd been a bone of contention between them. He thought he was old enough. Maybe he was. Maybe she babied him too much, overprotected him. Farm life was different for kids. Several of his friends drove tractors already.

But Austin was likely the only child she would have,

because she sure wasn't getting married ever again, so she probably clung to him too much. She would only have him for eight more years before he was a man, and she'd pretty much been mother and father to him since her ex left. If Austin really did get to fly to San Diego to visit his dad, Annie would be amazed, because he made a lot of promises he never kept.

At least Mitch didn't interfere. He told Austin to slide over, then squeezed himself next to her son. After the first jerk to get the chain taut, it was a smooth, slow ride into the shed. She wondered if the truck really could be fixed. How did he get parts for a nearly sixty-year-old vehicle?

"Is this home for you? The Red Valley?" she asked him as he crouched to unhook the chains from his truck. Austin had taken off with his dog, an Australian shepherd named Bo, who loved to chase the chickens, satisfying his herding instincts.

"Yep." Mitch moved to the tractor. Her gaze dropped to his rear as he crouched down again.

She could stare at that fine feature all day. The rest of him, too. Broad shoulders, narrow waist, slim hips. All man. She deliberately looked away. "Why were you in Argentina?"

"For work."

Great. Now he'd decided to act more like a cowboy and go almost silent. "Cattle, you said."

"The opportunity came up. I went."

"Is your family still living in the area?"

"Yep. We're not estranged. I'm just kinda independent."

"Stubborn, you mean?"

He smiled at that as he stood, chains in hand. Using

his wrist he tilted his hat back a little. His teeth were white and straight, his lips tempting. "Some have said so."

"So, you've worked cattle. Have you farmed?"

"I've picked up a lot of life skills along the way. I'm thirty-six, in case you're wondering."

"I'm thirty. In case *you* were."

He nodded but didn't comment. No flattery. No, "you sure don't look your age" compliment. Did she look older? Worn-out? Technically she should, since she was tuckered out from stringing her little farm along, hoping to turn it into a thriving enterprise again, needing to make enough money to live on with a few more comforts than they had now, which were pretty much nonexistent.

Mitch reached into the truck. "If I could stow my gear, I'll get started on the old greenhouse."

"I'll show you which room is yours," she said, walking beside him. "Austin, grab some gloves so you can help with the demo work. We'll be right back."

Annie led the way down the narrow hallway, pointing out Austin's room and her own, then Mitch's. It was beyond sparse, containing only a double bed, a dresser and a lamp.

"It's not much," she said, no apology in her voice.

"It's fine. Don't need more'n this. Thanks." He tossed his duffel on the floor next to the bed.

She moved into the doorway, blocking his exit. He cocked his head. His mouth curled up on one side.

"Ma'am?" he said politely, pointedly, his eyes taking on some sparkle.

"I'll be needing you to dump the contents of your bag onto your bed."

The smile left his face. He crossed his arms. "That would be an invasion of my privacy."

She moved into the room, shutting the door behind her in case Austin came flying in. "No. This would be your background check."

Chapter Two

Mitch didn't have anything to hide, but her command annoyed him nonetheless. Hell, he was doing her a favor, not vice versa. Although, to be fair, she didn't know that....

He refrained from jerking the bag open, acting casual instead. He lifted out the contents. First, five pairs of Wranglers, the same ones he'd been wearing since he left home, so they were a little worse for wear. Then four T-shirts, four long-sleeved shirts, an extra pair of boots, swim trunks, socks, briefs, belt, gloves and a couple of different weight jackets. Nothing fancy. He'd lived as a gaucho, although he'd been employed by one progressive ranch, not roaming the plains looking for work as many did. He hadn't needed possessions beyond the basics.

Mitch pulled out his shaving kit, unzipped it and passed it to her. Nothing was American-made, so the words were in Spanish, but each product was recognizable, including a strip of condoms, which brought color to her face when she pulled them out.

"Safety first," he said, enjoying her discomfort. "They're not for show. I always use 'em." The last thing he'd wanted was to deal with an unplanned pregnancy in a foreign country—or anywhere else, for that matter.

"That's important," she replied a little stiffly, uttering her first words since he'd started unpacking. She examined the empty duffel bag, checking for anything he might have tried to hide, he guessed. There were no pockets, no hidden contraband.

"I don't do drugs, Annie. Never have."

"Are you a drinker?"

"I like a cold beer now and then." He'd done his share of drinking when he'd first arrived in Argentina. Still grieving his grandfather's death, he'd sought oblivion from the pain, but it hadn't taken him long to see how stupid that was. Granddad would've knocked him alongside the head for hanging on to his grief—and his guilt.

"You and your son are safe with me," he said calmly as he transferred his clothes to the dresser, getting past his resentment, glad she hadn't been stupid about the situation, after all. He almost felt Granddad patting his shoulder. "You're welcome to check out my truck, too."

"Thank you." She opened the bedroom door.

"Like I had any choice," he muttered under his breath as he followed her out. He'd lived in the Red Valley forever, not counting the past three years and during college, coming home to work the ranch during summer breaks. People knew him, trusted him. It was strange not to be trusted automatically. Although, maybe he would've been if he'd given her his last name.

Outside, Mitch attached a long, low trailer to the tractor and drove it up to the demolished greenhouse.

The new structure she'd bought was lighter, and could be erected by one person, according to the packaging. High tunnel greenhouses had become familiar sites in farm country over the years, their Quonset-hut appearance easy to spot, their walls made of almost-clear plastic covering, a less expensive option to the old-style greenhouses.

The three of them hauled debris all afternoon. The dog and chickens got in their way frequently, but the atmosphere was congenial. Mitch caught Annie looking at him now and then. Whether she was taking his measure as a worker or giving him the eye, he didn't know. He just hoped she wasn't catching him doing the same thing in return. She was physically strong, able to carry much more weight than he'd anticipated. And she was tenacious, stopping only for a drink of water now and then, making sure that he and Austin did the same.

"What are you gonna plant in your new greenhouse?" he asked during one of their water breaks.

"Specialty potatoes and baby lettuces. I'll get most of my seedlings started in there, too."

"There's a big market for baby lettuce?"

"An incredible one, especially organic. And a fairly new clamoring for organic flowers."

"Who buys those?"

"People who care about the chemicals being used by the big international growers, which is where a large percentage of the flowers sold in this country come from."

Austin piped up. "I pick off the bad bugs."

Mitch knew all about organic, humane cattle ranching. His family had pioneered it, one of only a handful in the country who were certified. But flowers? "No one eats flowers."

"Sure they do," Annie said. "The upscale restau-

rants—and a lot of home cooks—use certain flowers
in salads all the time. But mostly I'm talking about table
flowers, not edible. Whether or not we eat them, we *handle* them. If a restaurant is going to all the expense and
trouble to provide chemical-free food for their customers, shouldn't their table flowers also be organic?" She
drained her water bottle, set it aside, then tugged on her
gloves. "My goals were taken into consideration when
I applied for a federal grant for the high tunnel and got
it. I want to build a standard greenhouse, as well. But
first I need to prove I have enough business to warrant
it. I'm not certified yet, but I'm working on it. I'll succeed. I have to."

"I gathered that," he said, then shook his head. "Flowers. Who knew?"

She smiled, which took years off her face. "You probably don't make a habit of decorating your dining room
table with a bouquet."

"How'd you guess?" He set his bottle next to hers.

"I didn't know how successful the flower business
could be. I found out by accident when I worked the
farmer's market for the first time last year. I brought a
bouquet from the yard to decorate my stall. It was the
first thing that sold. The next week I took along as many
as I could put together. They all sold. This year I made
it an official crop." She pointed toward the back of her
property. "I've got all that acreage out there that's not
being used. I'm thinking about having a real flower farm
after I'm certified."

"You're ambitious," he said as they carried a long,
unwieldy beam together.

She nodded but didn't add anything. The determined
look on her face said more, however. He wanted to dig
deeper and find out why, to understand. He'd never had

to start a new venture on his own, had always known what his place in life would be.

And had sometimes fought against it.

He'd never struggled like Annie, although he'd often worked long, hard hours and fought Mother Nature on plenty of occasions. He'd been bone-weary, ached from head to toe and wished he was anywhere but on a horse chasing stray cattle, but he also loved it. Couldn't imagine himself being anything but a cattleman.

Around six o'clock, Annie went inside to make dinner. The old greenhouse was mostly taken care of, split into two piles, reusable and trash. The salvageable items would be stacked in the barn, the rest hauled to the dump.

Mitch opened the hood of his truck, which brought Austin and Bo over to investigate. Austin climbed up on the bumper and looked inside, mimicking Mitch.

"What'd you think is wrong with Lulu?" the boy asked.

Mitch fiddled with various parts. "There's some rust from sitting for so long. Could be that's all it is, 'cept I drove her about fifty miles before she conked out. The gas is fresh, but the oil isn't. Know much about engines?"

"Nope. Mom's always mad if something goes wrong with our truck because she can't fix it. Too many computers in it or something. She calls it a con...cons something."

"Conspiracy?"

"Yeah. She's pretty funny when she's mad."

Mitch enjoyed that image for a minute. "She fixes trucks?"

"Her dad taught her when she was a kid. She fixes

everything. Or tries to, anyway. Repairmen are not in our budget."

The way Austin said that made Mitch smile. "Your mom seems like one mighty strong woman."

Austin shrugged. "She cries sometimes. At night. In bed. When she thinks I can't hear."

The thought twisted Mitch's gut tight. "Farming's hard work."

"Yep."

"For you, too," Mitch added, fiddling with a belt.

"I can handle it."

The grown-up way the boy said the words got to Mitch as much as hearing that Annie cried sometimes. Once again, it reminded him of how simple his life had been in comparison. He'd always known there would be hearty food on the table and a solid roof over his head.

Mitch gathered his tools and started pulling parts. He explained the function of each piece to Austin and let him handle them, showing him how they fit together to make a working unit. Bo padded over and sniffed Mitch now and then, giving him a good stare with his direct blue eyes, finally lying down between them as they worked. Then a chicken came into view, taunting him, and the dog was off and running.

The peacefulness of the moment struck Mitch after a while. He couldn't remember a time like it, except— Mitch swallowed around a lump in his throat. Except when he was a kid and his grandfather was teaching him how to work on the truck. It was their time, uninterrupted by chores or other demands. The bond they'd forged because of that time together never once weakened.

After a few minutes the screen door creaked open. "Dinner in five," Annie called out.

"That means come in and wash up," Austin said.

"Think we're having chili?" Mitch asked as they climbed the front porch stairs.

"That or omelets."

But the scent that hit Mitch when he opened the door was of frying onions. His mouth watered. "Smell's great," he said, leaning a shoulder against the kitchen wall, waiting for Austin to finish up in the bathroom before taking his turn.

"Cheese omelets," she said. "Fried potatoes and onions, sliced tomatoes. Plenty of bread, too."

He spotted an electric bread maker on the counter. She must've put the ingredients in earlier.

"Anything I can do?"

"It's under control, thanks."

Mitch watched her turn out a large omelet onto a plate, then she pulled two plates from inside the oven, with smaller omelets already on them, and started piling them with potatoes and onions. She knew her way around her kitchen, her movements smooth and practiced. His gaze landed on the apron bow that rested just below the small of her back, inviting a playful tug, he thought, then a sweep of his hands over her smooth, tight rear.

She glanced over her shoulder at him. He turned to one side, the doorjamb blocking her view before she could notice he was getting aroused. That would be the quickest way to be sent packing, for sure.

"Thanks for your patience with Austin, Mitch. He's a very curious boy. I know he asks a lot of questions."

"He's a good kid. You've raised him well." *He hears you cry during the night, and he worries about you, is protective of you.* "He told me you can fix just about everything."

"'Necessity is the mother of invention.' I'm grateful for the internet. I can pull up instructions on how to do most anything."

"Then why'd you need a handyman?"

"Muscle. Can't get that online, can I?"

Austin came running down the hall and took a seat at the table. Mitch didn't spend a lot of time cleaning up, either, anxious to dig in. The omelets were light, perfectly cooked, the bread fresh and hot, no butter necessary, which was a good thing, since she hadn't put any on the table. The potatoes and onions were browned and mouthwatering.

"I'd forgotten how good a tomato can taste," he said.

"From vine to table in ten minutes. Can't get better than that," Annie said.

Mitch saw her shoulders drop, her face smooth out, and was glad for the visible signs of relaxation. "What do you do after dinner?"

"We commune with nature," Austin said, grinning.

Annie swatted him playfully. "We chase the chickens into their roost. Actually Bo herds them, and we shut them in. After that we tidy up the grounds, do a little raking, that sort of thing. Then we sit on the porch and admire our land."

"Or play video games or watch TV," Austin added.

"And I have lots of computer work to do. Then we're in bed pretty early."

"The life of a farmer," Mitch said.

"And ranchers," Annie said.

"Definitely. So, who does the dishes?"

"Mom washes. I dry." Austin stood and gathered plates.

"How about if I dry tonight?" Mitch suggested.

Annie zeroed in on him, wondering why he would

volunteer to help with dishes. Because it would put them close to each other? She hadn't missed all the looks he'd given her while they'd worked.

"Unless there's a chore you want me to tackle instead, boss?"

Boss? She saw his mouth twitch just slightly. She was also aware of Austin waiting for her answer. Drying dishes wasn't his favorite task. "If you feel like raking, Mitch, I'd be happy to turn that task over to you."

"No problem." He took his own plate to the kitchen, winked at her, then left the house.

She let out the breath she'd been holding. The man was easy to be around. Too easy—except for the feelings he stirred inside her, dead so long she'd forgotten such feelings existed. Those weren't easy at all, creating a complication she didn't want or need.

At least he uses condoms.

The thought made her smile.

"What's so funny, Mom?"

She rinsed a handful of silverware and passed them to Austin. "I just feel good."

"It's Mitch." Austin nodded sagely. "Even Bo likes him, and Bo doesn't usually let strangers near me. I hope he's around for a while," he added in almost a whisper, as if wishing it out loud would destroy the possibility.

"Can't afford him for long, honey. Sounds like he doesn't stay in one place for any amount of time, either."

"I know. Why doesn't he tell us his last name? Do you think he's hiding from someone?"

"I don't have an answer for that, Austin. He must have a good reason."

Done with the dishes, she nudged him with her hip until he smiled.

"A day at a time," she said, crooking her pinky finger at him.

He hooked hers with his, something they'd done every day since her ex left. "Day at a time."

An hour later the evening chores were done. They sat on the porch, Annie and Austin on a glider, Mitch in a rocker. No one spoke for a few minutes.

"Your coop needs some repairs," Mitch said.

Annie pulled up a knee and wrapped her arm around it, staring at the horizon. "Yep."

"Got any chicken wire?"

"Nope. So far they haven't figured out they can escape. It'll have to wait until the new greenhouse is up. That's my priority. That's my income. The chickens just help keep us fed."

"I'd be just as worried about something else getting in. Foxes, even wild dogs, valley coyote. Even a cat could cause damage."

Annie's heart sank. Of course he was right. She hadn't even considered it.

"Chicken talk," Austin said with a sigh. "Can I go play video games instead?"

"Sure."

He disappeared inside almost before she said the word.

Mitch stretched out his legs, crossing his ankles, looking comfortable. "You mentioned something about expanding your flower beds into the acreage behind the orchard. Is that something you plan to do this year?"

"Probably not. I'll leave it as is, in case I need to sell part of the property to stay afloat."

"Can you sell just a portion?"

"I don't know. I haven't checked into it." She sighed.

"Two people tried to buy my entire property last year. I turned them down, obviously."

"Who were they?"

"Cattle ranchers. Shep Morgan and...I forget the other guy's first name, but his last is Ryder. You probably know them."

He shoved himself out of the chair and moved to the railing, his body stiff. "Did they pressure you?"

"Nicely, but yes. I continued to say no. Nicely. They seem to be rivals who seem to be on the same page."

"In what way?"

"They're waiting for me to fail. One of Morgan's sons pops in now and then, and asks if I need help with anything. Just being a good neighbor and all that. His name is Win. I see it for the ploy it is, since I discovered that the Morgans own the land surrounding mine."

Curious at how quiet Mitch was, she joined him at the railing so that she could see his face. "My ex, Rick, would've sold to them, but I bargained for keeping it as my part of the divorce settlement."

"Is this your only income?"

She didn't know why she was giving him so much personal information, except that he was easy to talk to. "Rick's faithful with child support. How about you? Do you have any kids?"

"No. I was married once when I was very young. It didn't last long." He eyed her. "Do you have a long-range business plan?"

She laughed softly. "Long, short and everything in between." She spent every evening on the internet searching out grant money, any way of making income that could help her hang on longer, until she could succeed on her own labors. She would have gone back to waiting tables in the evening to generate extra income, but she couldn't leave Austin on his own, and paying a sitter would cancel out her earnings. "I love this place. I'll do anything to keep it."

"There's no sense driving yourself to an early grave over a piece of land, Annie."

"Spoken like a vagabond. Well, I've been a vagabond. Roots are so much better." She shoved away from the railing. "I have work to do."

Annie went inside, her good mood having fizzled. What did he know about the need to own, to succeed? He didn't have a child to support and raise right. Who was he to give such advice?

Mitch hadn't come in by the time Austin went to bed and she'd showered and retreated to her own room. It wasn't even dark yet. She pulled down her shades, blocking the dusky sky. Usually she dropped off almost the instant her head hit the pillow.

Tonight she listened for sounds of him, the stranger she was trusting to treat her and her son right. After a while, she heard him come in, then the click of the front door lock. A few minutes later the shower came on. She pictured him shampooing his hair, which curled down his neck a little, inviting fingers to twine it gently.

Some time passed after the water turned off. Was he shaving? Yes. She could hear the tap of his razor against the sink edge. If they were a couple, he would be coming to bed clean and smooth-shaven....

The bathroom door opened and closed, followed by his bedroom door. After that there was only the quiet of a country night, marked occasionally by an animal rustling beyond her open window. She'd finally stopped jumping at strange noises, had stopped getting up to look out her window, wondering what was there. She could identify most of the sounds now.

And tonight she would sleep even better, knowing a strong man was next door. She could give up her fears for a while, get a solid night's sleep and face the new day not alone, not putting on a show of being okay and in control for Austin.

Now if she could just do something about her suddenly come-to-life libido, all would be right in her world.

Chapter Three

At five-thirty the next morning, Mitch climbed the porch stairs. He'd been up for a while, Bo joining him as he walked the property and made a list of what needed to be done, sorting through a personal dilemma at the same time.

His father wanted Annie's land. So did Shep Morgan. Morgan's interest was understandable, since he owned the land surrounding her property. But his father? His only reason would be if he wanted to use it as leverage for a deal later. Mitch's dad and Shep were both smart businessmen.

Ever since the gold rush more than a century and a half ago, the Ryders and the Morgans had ranched these parts, were stewards of this majestic land. Over time, however, cycles of drought, pestilence and the Great Depression had forced both families to sell much of their land. In the past forty years they had been buying back property, reclaiming their heritage and rebuilding their dynasties.

Theirs wasn't a Hatfield-and-McCoy-style feud, but a fierce, relentless competition for domination of land and cattle holdings.

And now they both wanted Annie's land. If she knew Mitch was a Ryder, she would send him packing, maybe even decide he was part of a ploy to get her land for his family. He wasn't ready to go home yet, but also she needed him—someone, anyway—to get her greenhouse operational, if she stood a chance at all to turn a profit.

The irony didn't escape Mitch. His father needed her to fail, and here Mitch was trying to help her succeed.

Except he couldn't see how she stood a chance of surviving another year financially.

Mitch carried his empty coffee mug into the house for a refill and came upon Annie standing in the kitchen perfectly still, staring straight ahead.

"Morning, Annie."

"You made coffee."

Crap. He'd screwed up. Maybe she kept coffee for a special occasion. Maybe the price was too—

"Thank you," she said. "This is going to sound maudlin, but no one's done anything for me for so long."

Honestly, he'd made coffee because he wanted some and didn't want to wait for her to get up. He didn't know what to say so he poured himself another cup, avoiding conversation. After a few seconds, he grabbed a mug from the cupboard and poured one for her. "How do you take it?"

"Black, thanks."

He finally looked at her face. She smiled. Her hair was freshly brushed, falling down her back in golden waves, reminding him of the Cinderella poster on his sister Jenny's wall when she was a kid, the one of Cinderella scrubbing floors, her mice friends around her, which Jenny preferred to the ball scene with the prince.

Annie leaned against the kitchen counter, the mug cupped in her hands. "You're up early."

"Always. What time does Austin get out of bed?"

"I let him sleep until six-thirty, more for my sake than his. I like a quiet start to the morning. Once he's awake, it's noisy. I generally fix breakfast around seven. If you'd like something to tide you over, toast or—"

"Seven's fine." What he'd *like* was to untie her robe and see what she was wearing under it, what she wore to bed, although he doubted she slept in the nude. "Stick to your regular schedule. I'll adapt."

Mitch pulled a folded-up paper from his back pocket and passed it to her. "I made a list this morning of what I could see needing fixing. Anything you want to add, just write it down. We'll get the high tunnel up today, provided it really can be installed in one day, as the literature says. I also came across some chicken wire in the barn, enough for three small patches anyway, which will do for a temporary fix."

"Where'd you find that? I thought I knew every nail and post stored on this property."

"Tucked behind some old boards covered in spiderwebs." He took a sip from his mug, stalling before he broke some bad news. "Um, are you aware there's a leak in your barn roof?"

She sighed. "Yes. Will a patch do for that, too? I can't swing a new roof yet."

"We can try."

"It's going to have to be you, not *we*. I don't deal with heights well."

He wasn't fond of heights himself, and that ladder of

hers looked pretty rickety. Apparently she thought he was a superhero who could do anything. He wondered how long he could stall the roof job. The chance of rain was slim at the moment.

"Had the place been abandoned for long before you got here?" Mitch asked, copying her stance of leaning against the counter.

"A year, but Rick's uncle hadn't been able to take care of it for a while before that, so no one had been working the land. It was a mess. It had taken Barney's lawyer a long time to find us, because we moved around a lot. Rick was surprised to be Barney's heir. He hadn't seen his uncle since he was a boy."

"Where had you been living?"

"When they found us? In Reno. We were both black-jack dealers, working different shifts."

"I can't picture that," Mitch said, more surprised than he let on. "You seem like Mother Earth."

"I took to this land instantly. I was so glad to get out of the casino, where you're barely aware of day and night, much less actual time. And then there's the noise and desperation. It got to be too depressing for me."

"I'll bet you were good at it, though."

"I make it a point to be good at whatever job I'm doing. I'm kind of fanatical about that. But this land? I'm willing to work my fingers to the bone to stay here, to raise Austin where he's outdoors a lot and in a real community, even if we have to eat beans most of the time. I'm finally home."

Mitch admired her determination but was worried about her, too. Someone that driven, that single-minded, often didn't see it was time to quit until they were broken, which made for a much longer recovery.

"Where'd you grow up?" he asked, sipping his cooling coffee.

"Everywhere—although always in cities. My parents moved all the time. I ended up marrying a man who lived the same way. By the time we landed here I was worn-out from it all, but more than ready to settle."

She was still worn-out, but in a happier way, he supposed.

"I'm going to go read the instructions on the greenhouse," he said.

"Really? A man who reads instructions?"

He leaned around her to set his mug in the sink, intentionally brushing her arm while trying to make it seem unintentional. She didn't move out of the way. In fact, she went very still.

"I'm out of my element," he said. She smelled good. Fresh. Female. "But I'm pretty good with my hands."

"I'll take your word for it."

He liked that she didn't let him get away with trying to unsettle her a little. He also liked that she seemed to have the same attraction that he did.

Although he had no idea what to do about it.

"There's a video on YouTube that shows a high tunnel being put together," she said. "I can pull it up, if you like."

"Yeah, sure. Thanks."

She found what she was looking for then stood behind him as he watched. He was completely aware of her. If he angled back just a little, his head would rest against her breasts. He'd already deduced she wasn't wearing a bra. On some women, that wouldn't matter much, but Annie's breasts swayed when she moved. At one point, she rested her hand on his shoulder and leaned closer to the monitor, the fluffy fabric of her robe brushing his ear. She pointed at something he couldn't see through a sudden burst of desire, which affected even his vision.

"This is the part that confuses me," she said. "Do we have to bend all those poles ourselves?"

The only reason he knew the answer was because he'd unwrapped all the parts and inspected them. "They were pre-bent at the factory."

"Oh. Good."

He turned around in the swivel chair. She didn't move away, not one inch. He decided he needed to have some amount of truth between them, to be honest about how she was making him feel. "You plannin' on keepin' this up, Annie?"

"What?"

"Puttin' yourself this close to me. Makin' me want you."

She stared back at him for a full ten seconds. "I didn't mean to. But I can't seem to control it."

He appreciated that she didn't apologize or make excuses or pretend innocence. "Well, if you want *me* to, you'd best be careful what you do. If you don't want me to control it, that's good, too. But I'd like to know where we stand on this."

Her voice was quiet, and a little shaky. "I haven't been touched in a very long time. And I'm attracted to you. That's a hard combination to ignore."

"You have a son in residence."

"Which will keep me on the straight and narrow."

"While I stay on the straight and up," he said, then watched her drop her gaze to his lap. "Every man has a limit to how much teasing he can take, even a man like me who was raised to respect women and to step away when she says no."

When she still didn't answer his question, he pushed

his chair out of range. "I think I need to watch the video again. Alone."

"I'll get dressed," Annie said in a rush, retreating, almost running to her room, where she shut the door and leaned against it, breathing hard. She hadn't recognized herself, coming on to him like that. She'd never been the instigator, having been rejected by Rick too often. They'd been almost strangers for the last few years of their marriage.

She covered her face with her hands, could feel the heat there, from embarrassment and desire. She'd wanted to drop her robe and climb onto his lap, to kiss and be kissed, to feel him, strong and sure, inside her. To feel desirable.

She was going to have to take big steps back, in thought and deed. As a single woman, she might be able to fulfill fantasies with him, but as a mother, there was no way. Austin was rarely gone, just an occasional afternoon movie with a friend from school, no overnighters, which was Austin's choice. He wasn't comfortable away from home overnight yet, although he'd had friends stay over with him.

Annie pulled on her jeans and boots. She grabbed a bra from her dresser and sighed. It used to be white, until she'd accidentally washed it with her jeans once. Now it looked gray and tired. She hadn't bought new clothes for herself in so long, just new things for Austin as he outgrew them. And occasionally Rick would decide to send Austin a care package, usually when he was feeling guilty about not following through on a promise. The box would be filled with clothing and video games, this last time even an iPod.

Dressed, she made her way tentatively into the living room, but Mitch was gone. Through the window she saw him dragging large metal poles over to the spot where they would erect the high tunnel.

She decided not to join him, even though it went against her work ethic not to be there helping. She figured he wanted some time alone.

How long will you stay? she asked him silently. Would he give her notice before he left or just take off? They'd only agreed on a few days, no more than a week. She couldn't afford him for longer than that.

So. Get Austin to the movies with a friend and enjoy this opportunity with a man who wants you.

She shoved her hair back, pulled it into a ponytail so hard it hurt. Who was this Annie Barnard, thinking about having a onetime fling with a drifter whose last name she didn't even know?

He comes with condoms.

She finally laughed at herself. She was a woman in the prime of her life who'd been denied intimacy for far too long, and it was manifesting itself by turning her into some kind of…tart. That made her laugh harder. She dropped onto the couch and buried her face in her hands, stifling the sounds.

"Are you okay, Mom?"

She felt the grin on her face as she looked up at her son, all sleepy-eyed and adorable. "I am A-okay."

"It kinda looked like you were going crazy."

"In a good way." She pulled him into a big hug, then offered her pinky. "A day at a time," they said in unison.

"Where's Mitch?"

"Outside, I believe. He's anxious to get started on the high tunnel."

"Me, too!"

"Then I'll get breakfast going so we can do just that."

Breakfast was scrambled eggs plus oatmeal with

blueberries from their garden. Annie was grateful that Austin filled the dead spaces in the conversation, as Mitch said little. Then they all headed to the yard and the immense project awaiting them.

Maybe one person could have erected the structure, but it would have taken days. By dinnertime, there was still work to be done, even with three of them working almost nonstop on it. But the construction went smoothly and would be finished by the next day. Then there would be end walls to construct and water lines to update from the old greenhouse remains—if they could be salvaged.

Annie was beyond pleased. She sat on the porch late in the day, sipping water and admiring what they'd accomplished so far. If Mitch had to leave now, she and Austin could finish it. Her relief was beyond measure, as the greenhouse was a huge part of her future success.

Yes, there were a lot more projects that needed attention, but none as important.

With Austin inside computer-chatting with a friend, she closed her eyes and pushed the glider with her toes until she heard Mitch's boots as he climbed the stairs.

"Good day's work," he said, not sitting beside her, not sitting at all, in fact.

"Tremendous. We couldn't have done it without you."

"Teamwork." He looked out over her land. "It's peaceful here."

"It took me a while to get used to," she said. More than a while, especially after Rick left and it was just her and Austin. The isolation occasionally got to her. Although she was friendly with a few people in the area, she didn't have a true girlfriend yet. For one, she was too busy. Then it also cost money for gas to head to town to have lunch now and then, not to mention the price of the lunch.

Her only real social time was on Monday nights at the farmer's market.

"Someone's coming," she said, sitting up at the sound of a vehicle turning into her road.

"I'm not ready for anyone to know I'm back yet," Mitch said.

"Okay." She wasn't sure she should be protecting him, but for the moment, she would.

He jogged over to the shed where his truck was stored, shutting the big doors to block the vehicle from view inside.

A truck with a Morgan Ranch sign painted on the door pulled up. Win Morgan got out and sauntered over to her. He was younger than Annie and looked much like his father, Shep, who'd tried to buy her land. His brown hair and eyes might be commonplace, but his face wasn't. He was about the handsomest man Annie had laid eyes on, especially when he smiled, like now.

"Evenin', Ms. Barnard," he said, all slow and charming.

"Mr. Morgan."

"Now, I told you to call me Win." He'd eased his way to the bottom of the steps. She didn't go down to greet him, didn't want to give up the advantage of height. "I was in the neighborhood and thought I'd stop by and see if you need anything."

"I appreciate the offer, but everything's under control."

"I see that. I'd heard through the grapevine that you got yourself a high tunnel and thought I'd offer to help you set it up, but I see you've already done it."

There was a question in his words but not his inflection, so she didn't answer him.

"Still don't trust my motives, I guess," he said with that charming smile. "Takes a while for a city girl to figure out we do things differently here. We help each other."

"I *have* heard that. I just don't need any help at the moment. But thanks."

The screen door burst open. "Mom! Ben wants to—" He stopped, seeing Win. "Hi."

Annie prayed Austin wouldn't mention Mitch, but at the same time she didn't want her son to lie for him, either. "Do you remember Mr. Morgan, Austin?"

"Sure." Austin lifted his chin in acknowledgment. "How's it going?"

"Good," Win said. "Nice to see you again."

Austin looked around. "Where's—"

"What does Ben want?" Annie asked, diverting her son.

"For me to go bowling with him. His mom would pick me up and bring me home. Can I?"

She didn't want to discuss specific times, since Win would then know when she would be home alone. "We'll talk about it later. Right now you need to finish cleaning your room."

He frowned but obeyed.

"I wouldn't harm your son," Win said, also frowning. "Nothing wrong with being friendly."

"Your father put a lot of pressure on me to sell, which didn't sit well. I'm suspicious of your offer of help—for good reason. Maybe in time I'll relax about it."

"Good enough." He touched the brim of his hat in farewell, then he was in his truck waving a final goodbye.

Mitch moseyed over. "Thanks."

She crossed her arms. "Why the secrecy?"

"My dad will want me back working at the family business. I want a little vacation between jobs."

She laughed. "*This* is a vacation?"

His smile was crooked. "I've always considered a change of scenery to be a vacation. Hard work doesn't bother me. I wouldn't know what to do with idle time, anyway. In that sense, this is a vacation."

"As long as you're not hiding from the law."

"No, ma'am. Not me."

She decided he'd used the word *ma'am* to show he was serious and accepted that at face value. "You must be pretty well-known, since you got out of sight even before you knew who was coming up the drive."

"As I said before, born and raised here." Mitch came up beside her on the porch, close enough to touch but not doing so.

"I can't ask my son to lie about you. He may very well tell his friend Ben, and therefore his parents, since he may be going bowling with them. In fact, I'm sure he would say something."

Mitch shrugged. "If it happens, it happens. It'd just be sooner than I want."

"I'm done," Austin said as he pushed open the screen door and joined them.

"Thanks, honey. Now tell me about the invitation."

"Tomorrow right after lunch. Ben's big brother will be there, too. He's thirteen. Their mom's gonna do errands then come back and get us."

Mitch wondered why Annie was hesitating. Because she kept her son tethered? Was she afraid to let him go somewhere without her? Because she didn't know this boy Ben's family well enough?

Because with Austin gone, they would be alone?

Mitch decided that was wishful thinking on his part. Attraction didn't mean action. They were adults. They could control themselves.

Unfortunately.

"Pleeease," Austin begged.

"Okay."

She'd barely gotten the word out when Austin leaped into the air, spun a hundred and eighty degrees and opened the screen door, all at the same time.

Mitch smiled at his exuberance. "He must love bowling."

"He's never been before," Annie said, staring at the door. "I think he's happy to be getting out of some work."

"I get that. I always had to work, too. Not much downtime, even during summer breaks. I missed my friends a lot when school was out, even with five brothers and sisters."

"Five? Wow. I have a brother somewhere. He stopped communicating about ten years after he had a big fight with our parents. I really miss him."

"Do you see your parents?"

"Now and then. They're still moving from town to town, job to job. At the moment they're in Florida working as campsite hosts. Rick's parents are AWOL, too. Austin's never had a chance to know his grandparents. Every time you talk about your grandfather, I feel sad for Austin."

"He was my best friend," Mitch said, but not wanting to talk further about him. "Need help making dinner?"

"Is that code for *I'm hungry?*"

"Maybe."

"I'll get it started."

"I don't mean to rush you." He grinned, belying his statement. He'd been hungry for a couple of hours.

She laughed and went inside. He followed, intending to use the bathroom then see if he could fix the chicken coop before dinner. As he walked past the computer, he saw the boy Austin was talking to via Skype. They were exchanging energetic dialogue about video games and levels and blasts. In the background a woman walked by. Mitch stopped and stared as she came closer to the screen and waved.

Stunned, Mitch backed up as she spoke.

"Hi, Austin! See you tomorrow."

"Okay! Thanks for inviting me."

"You're always welcome, sweetie."

"Something wrong?" Annie asked from behind him.

"That's Ben's mom?" he whispered.

"Yes, Marissa Mazur. Do you know her?"

Mitch faced her. He wondered whether it was an omen or just fate laughing at him. "Pretty well, yes. She's my ex-wife."

Chapter Four

Annie tried to remember what she knew of Marissa. Had she spoken of an ex-husband? Their conversations had taken place at the boys' school, at PTA events and bake sales and back-to-school night, or when one of the boys was being dropped off or picked up. Brief conversations about nothing in particular.

"If she has a thirteen-year-old son," Annie said, "you must have been really young when you were married."

"Older than you were, I think," he said. "You're thirty and have a ten-year-old."

"Touché." She smiled, not taking offense.

"She was my only girlfriend. We'd started dating when I was a junior and she was a sophomore, then got married when I was twenty-one. It lasted a year."

"So, she's from around here? I got the impression she'd moved here fairly recently."

"She moved away before the divorce was final. I

heard she'd remarried and was pregnant. I hadn't heard she was back. But then, I've been gone."

"Does it bother you?"

"Let's just say our divorce was not amicable. What were the chances that Austin and her son are friends?"

"I can't ask Austin not to go, Mitch."

"I wasn't suggesting that." He shrugged. "Well, what happens, happens. It only means my father would know I'm back. Doesn't change anything."

Annie studied him, wondering why he didn't want to go home. He'd said he and his family weren't estranged, but something was keeping them apart.

"I'm gonna work on the coop until dinner," he said, then walked out the door.

She returned to the kitchen. She'd put up a large quantity of tomatoes last year and used one of her last jars now to make spaghetti sauce. While she worked, she considered Mitch's comment that his divorce wasn't amicable. Hers had been, or reasonably so. She'd wanted the farm and Austin, and Rick hadn't fought her on either, hadn't even asked for joint custody. He called Austin every so often, sent him "guilt" gifts, but otherwise had stopped being his parent.

When Austin was younger and less jaded, he'd cried a lot because of things his father did or didn't do. Now he was more philosophical about it, especially once she'd convinced him it had nothing to do with him, but his father's immaturity. She always said Rick loved him—and he did—but that he just didn't know how to show it.

If she gave Rick more credit than he deserved, that was okay. She only cared about how Austin felt.

She and Rick had parted ways with sadness but resignation. They were better apart.

So, what did "not amicable" mean? And why? Could

she ask Mitch about it or wait for him tell her when—or if—he was ready?

"None of your business," she muttered as she added herbs to her tomato sauce. Except—had it scarred him in a permanent way?

"*Really* none of your business," she said aloud. She'd gathered greens from the garden earlier and now ripped them into pieces for salad, uncomfortable with how invested she already was in the stranger.

She leaned around the kitchen door to speak to her son. "Time to wrap it up, honey."

"Hey, Annie!" Marissa shouted then came into the picture. "How're you doing?"

Annie wiped her hands on a kitchen towel as she approached the computer and crouched over Austin's shoulder. "Everything's going well. How about you?"

"We found out I'm pregnant. With twins. Surprise!"

Annie felt a twinge of envy. "Congratulations."

Marissa laughed. "Maybe. Hey, I'll see you tomorrow around twelve-thirty."

"Thanks for inviting him."

The screen went blank. "Go see if you can help Mitch with the coop, please. It'll be about a half hour until dinner."

"Okay."

Usually Bo was at his feet, but he'd already followed Mitch into the yard.

Annie plopped into the computer chair. Marissa had always seemed fun and upbeat. She was pretty, although she wore quite a bit of makeup and always had her hair fixed just so. But then, maybe Marissa thought Annie didn't spruce herself up enough.

She tried to picture Mitch and Marissa together. She

was tall and slender, when she wasn't pregnant, anyway. They would look good as a couple.

But looking good has nothing to do with being right for each other.

"For heaven's sake, stop obsessing," she muttered, returning to the kitchen, prepping the garlic bread and finishing the salad before she called them in, wishing she had some hamburger to add to the sauce.

By the time dinner was over, the dishes were done, and the chickens rounded up, they all landed in front of the television, worn-out.

"Thanks for repairing the coop," she said to Mitch.

"Won't hold forever."

"The story of my life." She smiled. "I should rename this place Superglue Farm."

Austin was channel surfing but laughed.

"Does the farm have a name?" Mitch asked. "There isn't a sign out front."

"The Barn Yard. I had to get rid of the old sign, there was so little left of it. Someday I'll build a new one."

"You've got plenty of wood from the old greenhouse," Mitch said. "Rustic is a popular look, I understand."

"You mean I'd be in style? Imagine that."

"Austin and I could build you a sign in the morning before we finish up the high tunnel."

"Don't forget I won't be here after lunch," Austin said earnestly. "And I don't wanna be too dirty before they come pick me up."

Mitch smiled, appreciating the ploy for what it was. He'd tried to get out of work when he was that age, too, had gotten just as creative. "Well, maybe we should go build it now instead, before you shower."

Austin looked toward his mother, as if she would get him out of it somehow.

But Annie only said, "I've got some outdoor paint in the barn."

"Aw, Mom."

Annie glanced at Mitch, her brows raised in question. He gave her a thumbs-up then a thumbs-down. She considered it for a few seconds then turned her thumb down.

Mitch was struck by the sense they were working as a team. Parenting. It took him a moment to come up with something to say to the boy. "I guess you've worked hard enough for one day. But as for tomorrow, you know you can take a shower after lunch. I'd planned on having you dig a trench for the water lines in the high tunnel."

"Me? But…you're the one with all the muscles!"

Mitch laughed. "Gotcha."

Austin dived at Mitch, laughing, too. They tussled a bit. Bo joined in, too, at first protectively then barking and hopping, as if playing the game. It took Mitch back to childhood, wrestling with his brothers, challenging each other.

Austin finally sat back, panting, rubbing his hands down Bo's fur as he panted, too. "That was fun!"

"Who wants dessert?" Annie asked, standing.

"We have dessert?" Austin's eyes went wide. "Or just peaches?"

"Sugar cookies."

Austin's arm shot up. "Me, Mom!"

Mitch mimicked him. "Me, boss!"

Austin finally found a TV program he wanted to watch. Annie was in the kitchen. Mitch had time to think. He should tell Annie his last name before she found out another way. If Austin talked about him and Marissa figured out her ex-husband was hiding out at the Barnard place, she would spread the word, maybe not maliciously but the result would be same.

On the other hand, if Mitch told Annie, she would jump to the conclusion that he'd been there on behalf of his father. Why else keep his last name to himself? He doubted there was anything he could say to change her mind about that.

Hell, he wouldn't believe him, either.

Not wanting to examine it further, he went into the kitchen. "Need help?"

He caught her crying, quietly, smiling unapologetically, dabbing at her tears. "Thank you for playing with Austin. He's missed out on so much, especially family life."

Mitch let her words sink in then came close, keeping his voice low. "I'm not going to be here long, Annie."

"Oh, I know. I *know*. It was just *fun* to see him like that. I know you're leaving."

Maybe he should go now, before the boy got too attached. He hadn't considered that. He'd just been enjoying him. "There are other places I can stay, you know. I could come back during the day and work, then not hang around. Then when the work's done…"

He let the words trail off, because he didn't know how to finish the sentence. He should be just as worried about the attachments *he* was forming as he was about Austin. And Annie, too, maybe. Although hers might just be physical.

"Marissa is pregnant with twins," Annie said into his swirling thoughts.

The Marissa he knew had never wanted kids— although he didn't learn that until after the wedding. "She'll have four, then?"

"Five. She has a daughter younger than Ben."

He realized Annie was watching him for a reaction. "Well, good for her."

She'd stacked cookies on a plate and poured milk for all of them. He picked up two glasses and headed to the living room. From that point, the evening was more subdued. Austin showered and went to bed when told. Annie went next.

Mitch couldn't deal with being within hearing range of her showering, so he went outside and sat on the glider. Bo came along, abandoning Austin's bed when he heard the front door open.

The quiet night washed over Mitch in soothing waves. It wasn't quite dark yet. The sun had set but the sky held a tinge of orange and purple. It would fade soon, too soon. He'd always loved summer evenings, the welcome cooling after a long day of being out in the sun.

She'd created a home. He understood why she was fighting so hard to keep it. He had a house he'd hadn't seen in three years, one he'd helped build and he'd missed it like crazy, but he'd figured he would appreciate it even more when he came back. Now he had a hankering to see it again, to sleep in his own bed.

He must have made a noise because Bo whined then set his head in Mitch's lap as if sympathetic. He hadn't felt homesick while he was in Argentina, just sick with grief, which had lessened in time, and guilt, which hadn't.

He'd been able to set aside his anger and disappointment when his marriage ended after a much shorter period of time, and had barely thought about Marissa for years. Now here she was, back in Red Valley, mother of three and pregnant with twins. He'd never known someone could change to the degree she had. Not even close.

Bo hopped up a moment before the door opened and Annie came out. Mitch stood, offering the glider to her.

She waved him off. "I just wanted to say good night."

"Night." He couldn't get rid of the image of her crying because he'd played with her son. She might be strong, but that didn't mean she didn't feel the same things every mother felt.

She didn't move.

"Something wrong?" he asked.

"I've been considering asking Austin to keep your secret."

Mitch moved toward her. "I appreciate that, but I don't want to ask him to lie."

"He wouldn't be lying, just not talking about you. There's a difference."

"Why would you do that, Annie?"

"Because I trust you. I think you must have good reasons for keeping your identity a secret."

"For the moment. Not forever."

"I understand that. I think we can enlist Austin for a short time."

Mitch considered it, but not for long. "I'm willing to let fate have her way."

"Fate's a she?"

"Isn't she? The three goddesses of mythology, if I recall ninth-grade English correctly. Anyway, we all know women control human destiny."

"We do?"

"Oh, yeah."

"Are you thinking about Marissa?"

"Not at all. Just life in general. From my experience, anyway. In relationships, women lead the way, therefore have control."

She leaned against the doorjamb and crossed her arms. "I'm going to take a stab at this—you have trust issues."

"I—" Did he? He'd known Marissa for years before

they got married, and she'd been hiding her dreams and desires all that time, not cluing him in on the important issues a couple should settle before they marry. "Maybe I do. How about you?"

"No, although I'm careful. I'm too tired to have issues of any kind." She smiled in a way that touched his heart, then she patted his chest lightly and went indoors.

He put a hand where hers had been.

He wanted to believe her, that she didn't have issues, but it couldn't possibly be true. He hadn't met a woman who didn't harbor secrets about herself. They always revealed themselves in time. Which hadn't stopped him from enjoying their company, but had stopped him from letting himself become involved in what might be considered a real relationship.

He wasn't giving up half of what he'd built ever again. Once burned, twice shy, that was his touchstone.

Mitch snapped his fingers at Bo to go inside with him. A shower would feel good. A back rub would feel better.

Spending some quality time with Annie in bed would be perfect.

And tomorrow they would be alone for a few hours.

Also tomorrow the truth about him might be revealed.

Maybe it was just all meant to be.

Chapter Five

Annie had been dirty before, filthy even, but never from head to toe like today. They'd dug trenches, tested water lines, redug and retested, delaying going inside for lunch until they were done with the messy, muddy work. Austin had been allowed not to dig, but sent to pick blueberries to give to Marissa as a thank-you gift. He'd made himself a sandwich and was ready to go.

"They're here!" he called out, racing to the greenhouse. "They're coming up the drive."

Annie didn't even attempt to brush herself off. She would've only been rubbing the muck in deeper.

"Come meet my friend," Austin said to Mitch, who exchanged a look with Annie before answering.

"Another time, bud. I need to stem this leak before we create a sinkhole."

Austin frowned. "But—"

"Ben will be back," Annie said as Mitch went deeper

into the tunnel, out of anyone's line of vision from the driveway.

"When they bring me home, okay, Mitch?"

"We'll see."

"They're waiting, honey," Annie said, urging her son toward the car.

"Well, aren't you a glamour shot waiting to happen," Marissa said, laughing, as Annie came up to her window.

"You think?" Annie held out her shirt like a tutu and curtsied. "I left my tiara in the safe."

Questions about Mitch crowded Annie's thoughts. She couldn't ask them, not even in a vague way. "You're not showing yet."

"I can't button my jeans anymore. I'm held together with rubber bands. Thank goodness for long blouses. All buckled up, Austin?"

"Yes, ma'am. Here." He passed her the bag of berries.

"My favorites, thanks, sweetie. I figure he'll be back between four and five, Annie. They'll want to play the arcade games for a while."

"Two treats in one. Have fun, honey." Annie waved at her excited son, who was already in deep conversation with Ben and barely gave her a second look. She smiled as they drove off. It was heartening to see him having a good time with friends.

"So, how was it?" Mitch asked from right behind her, startling her so that she jumped.

She pressed a hand to her throat for a second. "Don't sneak up on me like that."

"I didn't think I was. Lots of gravel to crunch around here."

"Um, so how was what?" she asked.

"Seeing Marissa, knowing we were married once."

"Kind of weird. Did you see her?" Annie asked as they walked back to the high tunnel. She felt…strange, being alone with him, knowing they would be alone for hours.

"I didn't even try."

"Are you curious?"

"I guess. Kind of." They stopped just inside the tunnel, both of them staring at the mess. "I found the leak and changed out the line."

So he didn't want to discuss Marissa. Annie would respect that, even though curiosity ate at her.

When the dirtiest work was done, she grinned at him. "I know we're not completely finished, but doesn't it look beautiful?"

He grinned back.

"I'll bet you're starving," she said. "I know I am. How about if I take a quick shower then put some lunch together while you take yours."

"Sounds good."

"If you go in through the back door, the washer and dryer are right there in the mudroom. I'll leave a towel there for you. Let's put our clothes outside to dry so we can knock off most of the dirt before I put them in the washer."

"You got it."

Annie was aware of his gaze following her as she walked to the house. They were alone. She could invite him to shower with her.

No. That was too bold, and so unlike her. He needed to make the moves…except, would he? She was the boss, and he seemed to have been raised properly. Maybe it came down to how well they withstood the sexual tension that had not just existed but overwhelmed from the first time they'd laid eyes on each other.

Annie left her clothes on the mudroom floor and walked naked to the bathroom, something she never did since she was always up, dressed and ready to work when Austin was home.

The force of the shower struck heightened nerve endings as she soaped up. Fantasies started, stopped, restarted and swirled in her mind. She toweled off, not bothering to wrap her towel around her as she went to her bedroom to dress, wishing she owned some sexy lingerie, just in case. Before she put anything on, she called out her window to him that the shower was his.

She dabbed a little perfume behind her ears and on her wrists before pulling on clean clothes, her skin sensitive to the drag of fabric. Without thought she left one extra button undone, showing a little cleavage in invitation as she made her decision.

She would sleep with him, because what if he left tomorrow? She didn't want him to go away without making love with him, without knowing what it felt like to be skin to skin, to feel his lips on hers, then on her body. To cherish his body in return. What were the chances of Austin being away from the house again anytime soon?

Now or never, she decided.

She went into the mudroom intending to hang their clothes outside, but he'd already done it. Grilled cheese sandwiches and tomato soup for lunch, she thought. Something quick and light, but filling. They could flirt over lunch, leave the dirty dishes on the table, lock themselves in her room until they were sated—or until four o'clock or so.

When the sandwiches and soup were on the table, she heard him coming down the hall—heard his boots, that is. Boots? Maybe they didn't have the same idea about how to spend their afternoon. She wriggled her toes inside her socks. Maybe he didn't want to seem presumptuous, so he'd gotten fully dressed.

"Smells good," he said, taking a seat.

Bo whined outside the front door.

"I hosed down the dog, by the way," Mitch said, picking up the first of two sandwiches. "Figured I'd do it before I cleaned up. That's why he's outside—and unhappy."

"Plus his boy is gone."

Mitch nodded. He was having a hard time keeping his eyes on her face. The V in her shirt went a little deeper than usual, deep enough that he could see smooth, creamy skin above her bra. He also didn't miss the floral scent of perfume, either. To drive him crazy, he figured.

Which was a ploy that worked. He was crazy in lust for her. She'd been wearing an old T-shirt while they'd worked in the mud, and sometimes her nipples would get hard, and it was all he could do to keep his hands off her. Visions of stripping away her shirt, tugging down her bra and settling his mouth on her never drifted from his thoughts as they'd worked. And every time she'd bent over, he ached to cup his hands over that tight, round rear.

The gap in her blouse was clearly an invitation.

"It's been a long time since I've had a good ol' grilled cheese sandwich," he said after a long silence where they both just ate steadily. "Comfort food."

She nodded, then broke saltines into her soup. It was something his grandfather had done, too. "What was the food like in Argentina?" she asked.

"At the ranch it was lots of beef and beans, only rarely fresh vegetables. When we went into town once a month or so, I ordered local fare, especially empanadas not made with beef. Soups and stews are popular. They don't have a particularly spicy cuisine, which I missed."

"Where'd you live?"

"In a bunkhouse. Just one of the guys."

"Why'd you stay there so long?" She put her fingers to her mouth. "I'm sorry. If I'm being too nosy, just say so."

He took a sip of iced tea. "My grandfather's death had hit me hard. He'd worked as a gaucho when he was in his early twenties and always talked about what a great experience it had been. I decided to go. Staying so long just sort of happened. It was physically demanding, and I was exhausted, so I didn't have time to mourn."

"I was never close to anyone like that," Annie said thoughtfully. "I saw my grandparents a couple of times in my life, and I've seen my parents infrequently since I became an adult. I won't let that happen with Austin. I know we'll be close forever. He'll know I love him and care about him."

Something you don't know yourself? Mitch asked silently. He might have issues with his father, but he knew he was loved. He couldn't imagine what it was like not to have support during the bad times.

Their plates were empty. He couldn't stall any longer, needed to tell her what he'd come to realize. And yet he did stall. He stacked the plates and bowls and carried them into the kitchen. He heard her walking behind him. As he set the dishes in the sink, she reached around him to add their empty glasses, her hand resting on his back. She wasn't so blatant as to press her breasts against him, but all he had to do was move his arm about half an inch.

Her perfume scented the air, subtle but provocative at the same time. He faced her, met her serious gaze. She seemed to be waiting for him to make the first move. "Annie—"

"This may be our only chance," she said quietly, intently.

He knew that. It was also why he couldn't go through with it. "It's not that I'm not interested," he began.

Panic filled her eyes for a moment, then she slid both arms around his neck and went up on tiptoe.

A dragon hiding deep inside him breathed fire that roared through his entire body. She was a glorious handful, as he'd anticipated. But he couldn't take her to bed, not while he was keeping secrets from her. She would be more furious because of that than denying her— them—the chance to make love.

She would feel used. After all she'd been through, he couldn't do that to her.

"You're holding back," she said, dropping her heels to the floor but leaving both hands resting on his chest. Frowning, she studied his face.

"It's not that I don't want you. I do. More than I can say. But this isn't the right time."

"Are you involved with someone else?"

"No." He wrapped his hands around her arms and moved her back. "You don't know me."

"So, tell me about you."

He was stuck. If he told her, would she believe he hadn't been sent by his father to woo her into selling her property? If he didn't explain, he was only dragging out the inevitable disappointment, maybe worse, that she would feel.

"Not yet," he said.

"It's not because you don't want me. You're still aroused."

Her directness forced him to continue a conversation he wanted to end.

"I'm with a beautiful, sexy woman." It went beyond that, and he knew it. He was already falling for her, breaking all his personal rules about relationships with women. "But it wouldn't be fair to you."

"We want each other," she said reasonably. "Today that's all that matters."

"No." He softened his tone. "It's not personal, Annie."

She laughed, a hollow sound. "Oh, of course not." Then she walked away, leaving him feeling like a jerk.

But better a jerk than a user.

Chapter Six

Later that afternoon, Annie warily approached Marissa's car, prepared for questions about Mitch, having no idea what her answers would be.

"Sorry we're late," Marissa said. "Ben was close to beating the machine's previous high scorer, and you know we *couldn't* leave then."

"Of course not," Annie said as Austin hopped out of the car and raced around to hug her.

"Did you have fun?" she asked.

"Mega."

"Thanks again, Marissa." Still edgy, she waited for Marissa to say something.

But she only said, "He's a pleasure. See you soon!" She waved and was gone, no questions asked. Annie noticed that Austin didn't ask for Mitch to come meet his friends, either.

Austin shoved his hands into his pockets and gave

Mitch a serious look when he approached a few seconds later. "I didn't tell Ben or his mom about you."

Mitch hid his reaction well behind a single word. "Okay."

"You're kinda hiding out here, aren't you?"

Mitch barely hesitated. "In a way. I don't want you to worry. You and your mom aren't in any danger, and I'm not in any trouble. I just need a few days without certain people knowing where I am. I'm sorry I can't explain it more than that."

"A few days? That's all?" He frowned at Annie.

"You've known that all along, honey. We can't afford anyone for longer than that."

He raced off to the house, Bo at his heels. The screen door slammed behind him.

"I'm sorry," Mitch said.

"It's not your fault. And don't stop being his friend and mentor just because he's angry that you're not staying forever. He's learning from you. Please continue that gift to him."

"I'll talk to him."

"If he brings it up. Otherwise, I think it's better to leave it alone."

He conceded with a nod. "You'd know best."

They finally made eye contact. After a few seconds, she sighed. "I apologize for pushing you this afternoon. You seem like a man who keeps his word, and I tried to make you go back on it."

"Apology accepted," he said, but with a twinkle in his eye that she couldn't interpret.

The chances of Austin being away from the house before Mitch left were slim, so why was he making light of what had happened? Because he wasn't going far and they would still have a chance to really be together? She hadn't been able to get a handle on whether he planned to stay in the area after seeing his family or move on again.

Maybe one of the things she liked about him was the mystery, the unknown, which kept her charged up some, anticipating. Wondering. Everything in her life had been so mundane, the same thing, day in and day out, with little variation.

That wasn't true now. Now she woke up revved and ready to go. She had help with the work, which lightened the load but gave her adult company, too, not just a boy, his dog and some chickens. She felt lighter, happier. Sexy, too. She hadn't felt desirable for a very long time. And Mitch sure wasn't faking his interest.

She came out of her stupor when Mitch waved a hand in front of her face. She almost batted it away for interrupting her thoughts.

"Maybe we should build the sign for the front of the property," he said. "That might draw Austin out to help, and he'll forget why he's angry. Let's do the hammering by the porch."

She liked the way he thought. They gathered wood, tools and paint. They'd hardly started when Austin joined them, wanting to help. Mitch let him saw the wood until he decided it was too hard. But he hammered nails and applied a primer then a final coat of bright white.

They put their heads together and drew up several signs on paper until they decided they'd hit on the right lettering style. The Barn Yard, it would say in big, bold, black letters, all caps, then framed with blue lines. They decided to paint the mailbox while they were at it. It was amazing how it freshened up the front of the property.

"We need to make U-pick signs, too, Mom. We should do them now."

"U-pick?" Mitch asked.

"We're opening up the farm for people to pick their own berries starting not this weekend but the next, and run it for about a month, or until the crops run out." She'd been told by the head of the farmer's market that having a U-pick would endear her to the community, something Annie wanted more than anything. "We'll have blueberries and strawberries at first. The blackberries need more time."

"I'm in charge of 'em," Austin said, his chest puffed out a little. "And I get some of the profits."

So, more wood was cut, painted and stowed in the barn. It was past their regular dinnertime when they finally stopped.

Mitch returned to the high tunnel to put in a little more work time. Annie headed for the kitchen. She found Austin and Bo curled up together on the couch watching a Disney show on television. She sat down next to him.

"That was very smart of you to figure out what you did about Mitch."

He didn't respond, didn't even look at her.

"I'm sorry you're upset, honey. I wish I could make things different."

"I know how you could," he said, finally making eye contact.

"How?"

"Get Mitch to marry you. He'd make things better around here. We'd have more money to spend."

Annie hid her surprise, although she realized she probably shouldn't be surprised. "There's no guarantee of that, Austin. And getting married requires falling in love. I've known him for two days. No one falls in love that fast."

"I did," he said low and gruff.

"What?"

"I love him. He's good to me, like a real dad."

Annie kept her cool, even though one of her biggest fears seemed to be coming true—Austin was becoming too attached. "Well, that's an entirely different kind of love than the kind that makes people want to get married. As for your father, he's doing the best he can." Which was a shame. He missed so much in his son's life.

"I can tell Mitch likes you. Just do that stuff that girls do. Flirt with him. Laugh at his jokes. You know what to do. You're a girl."

You mean I should get in bed with him? I tried and failed at that. "I think we just need to be happy we met Mitch and be grateful for his help. None of us knows what will happen in the future."

Annie held out her hand, her pinky finger crooked until Austin finally, reluctantly, hooked his with hers. "A day at a time," they said in unison.

Annie kissed his cheek and ruffled his hair. "Go wash up. You can help me make the salad."

"What else are we having?"

"Mac and cheese." She'd made the casserole early that morning and only had to heat it. She walked toward the kitchen.

"Mom?"

"Yes?"

"You'll try, though, won't you? To make Mitch fall in love with you? You won't get all cold and mean-looking like you do with other men and chase him off?"

Cold and mean? "I will be warm and friendly," she said, not promising more, but understanding what he meant. She did get cool around men, especially those Morgan and Ryder men who wanted her property. They could use all the charm available to them, and it wouldn't make a difference. If she ended up having to sell, she'd do her best to find a different buyer. Both of those families were vultures.

At the dinner table, everything seemed back to normal. Austin talked a blue streak about his afternoon at the bowling alley and arcade, Mitch asked questions Annie wouldn't know to ask about the games, and Annie simply enjoyed herself. Aware of Austin's desire that she flirt with Mitch, she had a hard time even looking at him.

Her body felt different now that she'd acknowledged her primal needs. Mitch only had to be within a foot of her and she tingled. She'd also begun to rely on him. He'd made her life a whole lot easier in just two days—and maybe a little more difficult, too.

The phone rang just as they finished dinner and were taking dishes to the sink.

"Good evening, Ms. Barnard. This is Jim Ryder."

Annie's spine stiffened. The cold meanness that Austin had noted crept in. Even aware of it, she didn't put any warmth in her voice. "Mr. Ryder."

Dishes rattled behind her. She turned around and saw Mitch straightening up the stack of plates he'd just fumbled.

"I have a proposition for you," Jim said. "May I stop by and tell you about it?"

"I'm not selling, Mr. Ryder."

"Please. Just hear me out. What harm will it do?"

She realized she shouldn't completely shut him down. As much as she hated to admit it, there was a slim chance she might need him one day. Plus, she wanted to fit into the community. He was part of that. "Fine."

A brief pause ensued, as if he were shocked, then he said, "How about tomorrow morning around ten?"

"All right."

"I'll see you then. Have a good evening."

She hung up, then didn't let go of the receiver. "Bad news?" Mitch asked, coming up beside her.

"Jim. His first name is Jim."

Mitch frowned.

"I told you I couldn't remember the first name of that rancher, Ryder. That was him. He has a proposition for me. He'll be here at ten tomorrow."

"I thought you didn't want anything to do with him or the Morgan family."

"'Penny-wise, pound-foolish.'"

"Meaning?"

"Who knows? Jim Ryder could be the man to bail me out one day. I can't ignore that possibility."

"That's probably wise."

"What will you do while he's here?"

"I think it'd be a good time for Austin and me to take a trip to the dump and get rid of some trash that's accumulated around here before you open up to the public for the U-pick."

"So, Mr. Ryder would recognize you?"

He waited a beat. "Yes."

She contemplated that then nodded.

"Is it okay for me to use your computer to order parts for my truck?" he asked.

"Absolutely." She'd password-protected what she needed kept private, like her finances, so that Austin wouldn't see anything she didn't want him to see. "You don't even have to ask."

"Thanks."

Annie sat on the porch glider reading after dinner while Austin and Mitch played catch, Bo running back and forth between them. Too normal, Annie thought. Temptingly so.

Even that thought, and the fact Austin was happier than usual, gave Annie pause. What was Mitch's background and why was he hiding it? Say what he would about not being in trouble, his actions didn't match his words. People hide for a reason.

And here she was, chasing him when she'd convinced herself she didn't want a relationship with any man, at least not until Austin was grown. He was her priority.

However…she was a woman, too. She had needs she'd forgotten about, or at least shoved into a locked compartment in her mind. All that hammering in her head now was coming from those particular needs knocking for her to open that door.

"Mom! Come play with us," Austin called out.

"I throw like a girl."

Both males grinned at her.

"Mitch can teach you. Then you can play with me after he's gone."

Silence came over the yard. Even the chickens stopped clucking. Annie closed her book and set it aside. "I don't have a glove."

"Neither does Mitch. I don't throw that hard. Yet."

Mitch explained what her wrist and elbow should be doing, how her fingers should be set across the seams of the ball, how her arm should cross over her body after the throw in the follow-through. No wonder she threw like a girl. No one had taught her the right way.

Mitch stepped back as she practiced with Austin. Despite Austin's words to the contrary, he threw plenty hard, especially to someone without a glove or experience or larger, tougher hands. She yelped and dropped the first ball he threw back to her.

"Throw the ball to me," Mitch said to the boy. "I'll pass it to your mom, and she can throw again."

He was a great kid, and perceptive, too, Mitch thought. The way Austin had protected him was remarkable for someone so young. They would have time tomorrow to talk while they made the trip to the dump. Mitch wasn't sure what he would say, but they needed an open dialogue.

Mitch understood what it meant to idolize someone. His grandfather had been his touchstone. And even as ornery as Granddad could be at times, Mitch always knew he was loved and accepted. He wanted Austin to have the same experience—but it couldn't be with him. That would come from whomever Annie married, because surely she would someday.

Mitch had been manipulated and lied to, and he'd learned from his mistakes. Until after the wedding, Marissa had never told him she didn't want children, nor had she even hinted that she didn't want to live on the ranch but in a city, with conveniences, especially shopping.

But she was more than happy to take half of everything he had, including the house he'd built. He'd only finished paying her share for that a few years ago. That is, repaying his father for the loan to pay her off.

It was easy to forget all that when he watched Annie play ball with her son. They laughed and teased each other. She was a good sport. Austin had a ways to go with that.

"Uncle!" Annie yelled after a while. "Bench me,

please. Where's the trainer? I need an ice pack for my shoulder."

"Geez, Mom, you only threw the ball, like, twenty times. You pick up fifty-pound bags of fertilizer, no sweat."

"I maneuver fifty-pound bags, not pick them up." She hooked an arm around his neck as they all headed for the porch. "How about pouring us all some lemonade?"

"Okay."

Annie plopped onto the glider. Mitch leaned against the porch railing, crossing his arms and taking a good look at her. "You're not really in pain, are you?"

"Not now, but I'll bet I will be tomorrow."

"Has Austin played organized sports?"

She shook her head. "It takes too much time and gas to get him to practices and games. He plays at school with friends, but that's all."

"You don't mind the isolation out here? Your nearest neighbor…?"

"Is on the other side of the road about a mile down. No, I don't mind it. Well, sometimes I do. Sometimes I get lonely." She shrugged. "Mostly I love it too much to let anything bother me for long. I'm just happy to be planted in one place."

"Is Austin?"

"Not as much as I am. He doesn't complain much, but it'll probably be different when he's a teenager. I hope by then my farm will be well established, and he can drive where he needs to go."

"What do you think Ryder will offer you tomorrow?"

"Money for something. It's the *something* I can't guess."

"And there's nothing at all he can offer to entice you?"

"Not that I can think of."

Mitch could only guess at the possibilities, too. At the least his father could offer it to Shep Morgan at a profit. Their unspoken competition for land dominance came at a cost for both of them, but didn't stop them striving for it.

Austin brought two glasses of lemonade then went back for his, sitting next to his mother.

"Did you play baseball when you were growing up?" he asked Mitch.

"Football. But I've got three brothers, and we played baseball together a bit."

"What position did you play on the football team?"

"Quarterback." It seemed like decades ago.

"Did you break any records?"

"A couple. They didn't hold for more than a few years before someone else broke 'em." The homemade lemonade was a perfect balance of sweet and tart. Mitch's mom made a mean lemonade, too. Suddenly he missed her. She was a strong woman, but took a backseat to her husband—unless she was exerting influence behind the scenes. "What sports do you like, Austin?"

"I like baseball the best. We play soccer at school. I'm pretty good at that. I'd try football, but Mom's afraid I'll get hurt."

"It's a rough game," Mitch said, although he didn't think that was a good reason not to play.

"Austin," Annie said.

"I know. I know. It's time for shower and bed."

She smiled. "You and Mitch are going to take a load to the dump tomorrow morning."

"All right!" His eyes lit up. He hopped out of the glider and hurried into the house.

"How can anyone like going to the dump?" she asked, shaking her head.

Mitch sat next to her. He could see the surprise in her eyes at his move. "Every mother I've met hates to have their son in football, or wrestling, for that matter. I understand from a parent's point of view. But I also would like you to know the positive side, at least for me, of football. I learned a lot by playing the game— how to lead, how to be part of a team, sportsmanship, logic skills. Not to mention how it helped with raging hormones. The aggression kept a handle on them. Most people don't think about that."

"And you were popular because of it, especially being quarterback."

"No doubt about it. I liked having that status, the respect that came with it."

"Did it get you girls?"

He looked away, remembering. "It got me Marissa, who was a cheerleader."

"Do you regret that?"

He gave it some consideration, but in the end there was only one answer. "Yes. It's colored my world ever since."

"Same here, except that I got Austin out of the deal, so no regrets for me." She touched his arm. "Thanks for the perspective on football. I know I'm overly protective. But I've got time to think about it, don't I?"

"Not really. Kids have to start young and develop their skills. They can't wait for high school to start playing. By then too many others have been coached for years. He's at exactly the right age now."

She sighed. "Maybe I could get a car pool together when the time comes."

"My guess is sign-ups are already going on. They generally start practicing before school starts."

"It probably costs a small fortune."

"The money situation can always be managed." He could work out a way for her. A boy needed to—

Mitch stopped the thought in its tracks. He had no business—and no right—getting involved. Maybe he shouldn't have said anything at all. Maybe he'd made it worse.

Austin hopped out onto the porch then stopped cold, seeing Mitch seated next to his mother. Then he grinned. He leaned over and gave his mom a hug, then did the same to Mitch.

"Good night!" he called then raced into the house.

Mitch stood. It was obvious that Austin wanted him to stay on, and maybe he even saw his mother and Mitch getting together as a way of that happening. Mitch wouldn't put it past Austin to be sneaking peeks at them on the porch to see what was going on between them.

"I'm going to work on my truck a bit before bed," he said. "Good night, Annie."

He should apologize for the abruptness of his leaving, but he didn't. He needed to keep some distance between them, although how that would be possible when his head was filled with the memory of her, the scent of her perfume, her willingness...

He needed all those skills he'd learned in football to stay strong, to keep his self-control.

Hell, maybe what he needed was a good game of scrimmage with his brothers to knock his hormones back into place.

He laughed as he reached the shed, running his hand over the familiar curve of Lulu's fender.

He'd rediscovered adolescence. Too bad he couldn't enjoy it.

Chapter Seven

Red Valley got more than its share of wind on any given day, but the next morning it whipped like crazy, blowing dust that cut through fabric, testing the limits of the high tunnel. Mitch stood in the yard, his eyes watering from the wind as he examined everything within sight.

"We've been through this before, many times," Annie said, coming up beside him, her hair whipping around her head. "There's always some damage, but I've been able to fix it."

"This isn't a good time to haul the trash." He had to shout to be heard.

"I agree. You can just stay inside when Mr. Ryder gets here. Make sure you don't have anything personal out, since I'll have to invite him in out of the wind."

"All right."

"Do you want Austin to stay in his room, too?"

A loud cracking sound had them turning their heads. The shed door had blown open, revealing his truck. They raced to it and together shut the door and bolted it, the latch too loose for Mitch's comfort. He couldn't do anything about it now, however, as some of her strawberry boxes upturned. They weren't finished righting them when a truck turned into the driveway.

Mitch jogged into the house, grabbed Austin by the hand, pulled him to his bedroom and told him to stay quiet and stay put until he was called. Then Mitch went to his own room, leaving the door ajar to allow him to eavesdrop.

A minute later wind whipped through the house as the front door opened and closed.

"I'm surprised you ventured out," Annie said. "It's not like this was a meeting that couldn't have been put off."

"I like to stick to my schedule."

Mitch heard his father's voice for the first time in three years. He leaned against the wall, and closed his eyes.

"Have you met my son Vaughn?" Jim asked.

Mitch came to attention. Vaughn was two years older than Mitch, the firstborn. And he was the ranch's attorney.

"You do look familiar," Annie said.

Hell, yeah, he looked familiar, Mitch thought. While they didn't look like twins, the resemblance between them was strong.

"I don't believe we've met," Vaughn said. "I'd remember, I'm sure."

Smooth-talking Vaughn. Mitch smiled. He'd missed his brother, all his siblings.

"Please, have a seat," Annie said.

Mitch could hear the tightness in her voice, could picture her stiff, defensive posture.

"First," his father said, "I want you to know I admire what you're trying to do. I'd be the same, unwilling to give up without the biggest fight of my life. I've been thinking a lot about you and your situation, and I'm thinking we could help each other. Vaughn?"

"We'd like to lease the acreage behind your farm. It would provide you with an income and give us room for more grazing land."

"I'm sorry you came out here for that," Annie said. "I have plans for that land."

"May I ask what they are?" his father said.

"I'm not ready to answer that."

"Perhaps we could combine forces."

"No, thank you. I think the legalities of that would be problematic for me. Again, I'm sorry you came out on a day like this."

"We only live twenty miles from here. It wasn't a hardship. Well, thanks for your time, Ms. Barnard. If you change your mind, please don't let pride stand in the way of getting in touch with me," his father said. "The offer doesn't have an end date. Yet."

"Feel free to consult an attorney of your own," Vaughn added. "Here's our offer in writing."

"That's not an expense in my budget."

"You choose the lawyer," Jim said. "We'll pay for it. We want you to feel comfortable."

"Thank you."

Mitch hadn't known Annie for long, but he knew what her tone of voice meant—go away. He'd bet she was standing tall and still, her hands folded in front of her, her expression steely.

He wondered what it would take for her to give up

on her dream? Bankruptcy? She probably didn't have a mortgage, since Barney would've inherited the place from his father. But even with all that equity, Mitch didn't think a bank would give her a loan, not while she wasn't bringing in enough income to repay a loan and still get by.

On the other hand, maybe the bank would, figuring they could recoup their money easily. His father and Morgan would be first in line to buy.

He felt sorry for her, having these two powerful men badgering her with their offers, trying to dazzle her with what must seem like a lot of money in her current position. She would like to offer Austin a better life, but "better" didn't have much to do with money, in her eyes. As far as she was concerned, they were already living a better life than ever before.

It was hard to entice someone when they didn't feel deprived.

Out of his bedroom window he saw his father and brother drive off, then he made his way to the living room.

"You heard?" she asked.

He nodded.

She passed him a sheet of paper, which he skimmed.

"I'd like your opinion, Mitch."

"I don't think you're ready to accept his offer." He couldn't comment on the price they were willing to pay, not without doing some research.

"I'm right, aren't I? I can do this."

He wasn't about to destroy her dream with his own speculation. "I know you need to try."

Mitch glanced out the window and spotted the shed door open, his truck visible. "When did that open?" he asked, barely above a whisper.

She joined him. "I don't know. I heard a noise a few minutes ago. Maybe then? Do you think they saw it? Would they recognize it?"

"Hardly a soul around here wouldn't." But did they see it or had they been focused on getting to their truck in the wind? From the porch it stood out like a beacon.

"Austin, you can come out now," Annie shouted down the hall.

"In a minute. I'm on level four," he called back.

"Oh, to be so easily distracted," she said, smiling, then she laid a hand on Mitch's arm. "Are you worried?"

"Fate will decide." He smiled to put her at ease. He hadn't intended to involve her in his problems. "It's too windy to work outside. Let's all play a game. It'll be like a ditch day from school."

They were in the second hour of a heated game of Monopoly when the wind died. They surveyed the property, cleaning as they went, tossing broken branches, righting tipped containers, making sure the high tunnel hadn't sustained damage, especially tears in the plastic film. Because she was using so many tall boxes for her strawberry plants in order to make picking easier for her customers, there was a lot of damage to them. If only they'd had time to move them into the greenhouse....

"We can salvage them," Annie said, coming up beside him. "This has happened before. And it wasn't bad for the table flowers. Blew all the stuff away that accumulates in the leaves. When we pick them on Sunday, they'll look great."

"Why Sunday?"

"I'll be taking as many bouquets as I can manage to the farmer's market on Monday. The flowers will survive in water for an extra day, but I like to wait until the last minute to pick the vegetables."

The chickens had ventured out of their coop, where they'd gone on their own to wait out the windstorm. They pecked the ground, finding new delights.

"Next year I'll stake tomatoes down the middle of the greenhouse. I want to specialize in heirlooms. They're harder to grow, but it'll go well with the organic appeal for the customer. I'll grow a lot of Roma tomatoes, too, since they're so good for canning."

"Do you have a master plan?"

She grinned. "Which one? I have a sketch pad full. I've been refining and refining after doing a lot of research and talking to other growers. I guess I've boiled it down to something workable for next year. That rectangular garden right inside the front gate? That's all pumpkins, my U-pick crop for the fall."

He studied her face as she looked over her land, seeing something he couldn't—the end result. "There are a lot of risks involved, aren't there?"

"Most of them out of my control. I think table flowers will eventually be my best bet, but it's going to take some trial and error to find the right flowers to sell." She dusted off her hands. "Break's over."

Bo chased a chicken, then two chased him, and everything was back to normal.

After a long afternoon of cleanup, they ate dinner and finished the Monopoly game. When Austin got in the shower, Mitch logged on to the computer to see if the parts he'd ordered for his truck had been shipped, but there was no email from the supplier. He scrolled through the rest of the messages, then just as he was about to log off, a new email arrived.

So close, yet so far away. Your mother misses you, son.

Of all the things his father could've said, that was

the most effective. No threat. No questioning what he was doing, why he was at Annie's. Just that his mother missed him.

I'll be home tomorrow, he wrote back before he could overthink it. He logged off. "I'm done," he said to Annie so that she could use the computer herself, then he went outside.

He'd known today after hearing his father's and brother's voices that he couldn't stay away any longer. The familial bond might have been tested while he was gone, but it hadn't broken, was never in danger of breaking. He'd decided to see his father as the enemy so that he could justify staying away, but he'd never been the enemy, just a roadblock.

Mitch wandered over to the shed, pulled on the overhead light. Parts were scattered on shelves in an order only he would make sense of. If the new parts arrived on Monday, he could wrap it up and move on. Move home. He would've been at Annie's for almost a week at that point. All the heavy jobs would be done, provided he worked up the nerve to climb the ladder to fix the barn roof. A raging bull caused him less trepidation.

"Hey, Mitch!" Austin called from the porch. "Good night."

"Night, buddy. Sleep well."

Austin hesitated. Was he waiting for a hug? He probably was barefoot and not allowed to walk across the yard right before getting into bed.

His shoulders slumped, he turned around.

"Hold on," Mitch said, then jogged over to him and up the stairs. He gave the boy a hug. Austin clung for an extra few seconds, then he rushed into the house.

Mitch rubbed his face with his hands. He hadn't known anyone could bond with a child that quickly, not someone else's child, anyway. His decision to pretend to be the handyman Annie had hired was weighing heavily now. Secrets were building upon secrets, attachments forming where they shouldn't.

The potential for hurt was increasing—that got to Mitch the most.

Annie came outside. The sun was just setting. "My favorite time of day," she said. "Except for dawn."

He didn't say anything, still lost in his own thoughts, but aware she was there.

"Everything okay?" she asked.

"I'd like to borrow your truck tomorrow, if I may. There's someone I need to see."

"That's fine." She cocked her head. "You're awfully subdued."

"Sorry."

"It was an observation, nothing needing an apology."

"I won't be here much longer, Annie."

"I'm prepared for that."

Am I? he wondered. Once he saw his father tomorrow, there would be no turning back. He'd be expected to rejoin the ranch crew.

"Just one thing," Annie said. "When you leave, does that mean you'll be leaving here or leaving the area?"

"Here."

"And your identity will no longer be a secret from me?"

"Yes." Although she wouldn't want to see him when she learned his last name was Ryder. Mitch was sure of that. Why hadn't he just taken her into his confidence from the beginning? Or when she'd told him his father had put some pressure on to buy her property?

His own selfishness had gotten in the way of good sense.

"So you're done drifting?" she asked.

"For now." He smiled at her, wanting to lighten the mood. What he really wanted was to pull her into his arms and kiss her senseless, not just to stop the conversation but to start something else. He couldn't, however. *They* couldn't.

The phone rang, ending the torture. From what he could overhear, he decided it was her ex.

"He's in bed, Rick." She used the same tone of voice she had with Mitch's father. "No, I'm not going to wake him up. You need to call earlier in the evening, you know that….Are you positive this time?…No, actually I don't have faith in you….School starts August 20, so how about the fifth? Then he'd have a week at home to get ready….I've told you before. You'll have to come get him and bring him home. He's too young to fly on his own, especially with a layover. Whether you fly or drive is up to you….Yes, I know it's a twelve-hour drive from where you live….I swear, Rick, if you disappoint him again—"

She had come to the screen door so that her back was to the house and her voice less likely to carry back to Austin's room, Mitch guessed. The phone cord stretched to accommodate her.

"You've seen him once in the past year. I think you can do this much for your son. I can get him to the Medford Airport….You do that. But please don't change your mind. He's expecting to see you. He's excited about it."

She hung up the phone then returned.

"Was he trying to back out?" Mitch asked.

"No. He loves Austin, I have no doubt about that. But he doesn't like being inconvenienced. It's a long trip— twice. I get that. But if the situation were reversed, I would do it. Every month, even. Of course, I wouldn't have moved away from my son in the first place."

Mitch couldn't offer words to her—it wasn't his place to comment on Austin's father—but he could offer comfort. He put his arms around her and held her. She relaxed before long, nestling closer, sighing. He didn't take it further than that, although he was tempted.

"Thank you," she said, pushing away, leaving in a hurry. "I'll go take my shower. Good night."

"Night."

"Oh. What time will you be leaving tomorrow?"

"Early. Right after breakfast."

"How long will you be gone?"

"Depends on a lot of things." Will it be a pleasant visit? A difficult one? Will his father demand something of him he wasn't prepared to give? Would his mother exert her own influence? "My cell phone should work somewhere along the way. I'll try to let you know, but don't worry if you don't hear from me. It won't mean anything in particular."

"All right."

The sky had darkened considerably, and his mood with it. He was anxious for tomorrow to come. He had a life he needed to start living.

Chapter Eight

Mitch forced himself to look around, to absorb all the sights of Ryder Ranch as he approached it then turned onto the long driveway to the property itself. His house was on the right, not visible, but shaded by a grove of oaks, mostly. Each Ryder child had been gifted a piece of property on their twenty-first birthday. Mitch had picked his spot when he was Austin's age. Although Vaughn was the oldest, he hadn't built until recently, when he'd decided to leave his law practice in San Francisco and come home again, his wife and daughter with him. Now he was a single dad with a happy grandma nearby to babysit.

Acres of grazing land surrounded the compound, although this wasn't the only Ryder property used for grazing. They owned many properties in the area and elsewhere in California, transferring cattle by truck to new ones frequently. This time of year they were grass-fed, which was ideal.

Because he was driving Annie's truck, he wasn't recognized when he pulled up to the main complex. He'd passed his parents' home on the left, a sprawling eight-bedroom house in which only his mother and father lived now. His youngest sister, Jenny, was a senior in college. Most of the rest of the siblings were scattered on the property. His brothers Adam and Brody were living in Mitch's house, since they hadn't built their own homes yet. He had to make a decision about letting them stay on with him or taking it back for himself.

He jumped down from the truck, excited and anxious. Everyone would be busy this time of day. There was always overnight business to tend to—fences needing repair, water troughs to maintain, strays to round up, endless chores done by rote after years of working the property.

No one came out to see who'd pulled up. He decided to walk to the family home in search of his mother. He'd taken only a few steps when he spotted her on the porch waving—and he was struck by how cruel he'd been to be gone so long, even though he would have been hell to live with had he stayed.

He ran to her, leaped up the stairs, picked her up and squeezed the life out of her. She was laughing and crying. He was swallowing hard. Dori Ryder was tall and willowy and very strong, in body and spirit. She was a rancher's wife, and a lot was expected of her.

"You've gone blond and sassy," he said, stepping back.

She finger-combed the short hairdo. "I've always been sassy."

"Yes, ma'am, you have."

She put her hands on his face. "I've missed you so much, Mitchell."

"I've missed you, too, Mom. I didn't even know how much until I started down the drive."

"Are you hungry? Can I fix you steak and eggs?" They walked into the house, where nothing had changed. Home.

"That sounds like heaven, except that I've eaten, thanks. Where's Dad?"

"Riding fence. I let him know."

They automatically went into the kitchen, her domain. She poured coffee without asking and passed him a mug, black.

"You look good, son. I don't know what I expected, but the time away hasn't hurt you."

"You don't think I look three years older?"

She looked at him over the rim of her mug. "You're a little more weathered, maybe. It adds to your handsomeness, but also makes you look a little more formidable."

He laughed at her flattery. "You've always been my biggest fan."

Her eyes sparkled. "I can still picture you at age two on your sweet old horse, Mabel, your hair sticking out from under your new hat. You'll always be that angel."

Out the window, he spotted a horse and rider approaching at a good clip then slowing as they neared the house. The horse's reins would be looped over the hitching post next to the porch. The tall, sturdy rider would stomp his feet four times, the way his wife had trained him then fling open the front door.

One, two, three, four stomps. Then boots crossing the living room. They'd torn down the wall between the kitchen/dining room/living room a few years back, modernizing the space, opening it up.

Mitch stood as his father approached, not slowing down, but pulling Mitch into a big bear hug. It was more than he'd expected.

"I'll take a cup of coffee, sweetheart," Jim Ryder said, then he settled on a bar stool, as did Mitch, who waited for his father to speak first.

"How come you've been hidin' out at the Barnard place?"

"I wasn't hiding. I've been helping her out."

His father's brows went up. "I call it hiding when you don't let your family—who haven't seen you in aeons—know you're back in town. And you hole up when I arrive. How'd you land there?"

"My truck broke down by her house. She mistook me for a handyman she'd hired over the phone. I didn't correct her, and I still haven't told her my last name."

"Mitchell Ryder," his mother said, shock coating the words. "How could you?"

"Surprisingly easily. I wasn't ready to come home yet. It was kind of a joke at first, then it wasn't so funny when I found out you've been wanting to buy her out."

"I'd be doing her a favor. There's no way she can make a living off that place."

"She's pretty determined."

"Determination can take you a long way, but in this case, not far enough."

"She tells me that Shep Morgan wants the place, too."

"Course he does. He owns everything around it. Barney would never sell it to him. Shep tried for years, kept raising the offer, but the old guy wouldn't budge. Ms. Barnard's ex-husband would've sold it, but she wanted it something fierce, I guess." He spun his coffee mug on the counter. "So, how've you been helping her? I noticed the new high tunnel. You responsible for that?"

"Only putting it up." Mitch was uncomfortable talking about Annie. No, *protective*—that was how he felt. He admired her, and he didn't want his father or anyone talking about her.

But Mitch also wanted his father's approval, had always wanted it and never seemed to be able to get it fully, unconditionally.

"In your opinion, can she last the winter?" his father asked.

The answer was no. Mitch knew it. Annie probably knew it. But she was resolved to try, and Mitch didn't want her to go down without a fight.

"I honestly don't know," he told his father. "Life's a mystery."

His father laughed at that. "It sure is. Take you, for instance. Out of all my kids, I never thought you'd be the one to take off like you did. Vaughn had different goals all along, but even he's back now. Adam and Brody are content here, always have been. They've taken on leadership roles, too. But, you know, I expected more from you than the others. Ranching was in your blood from the day you spun your first lasso. I think you were two."

"You were harder on me than the others." Mitch noticed his mother slipping out of the room, giving them privacy.

"I was."

"Why?"

"'Cause you're most like me. This ranch will need a leader when I'm done working it. That's you."

"Maybe Jenny or Haley will want the job." Even as Mitch made the suggestion that one of his sisters be in charge, he knew he was reaching. Haley was a physical therapist and loved it. Jenny was too sensitive. She always named the animals right after they were born and then was crushed when they were slaughtered. She'd become a vegetarian years ago.

"What do you want to be different this time around now that your granddad won't be here as our buffer?" his father asked.

"I'm tired of buttin' heads with you, Dad." He held up a hand. "I know you love me. I don't question that. But I'm thirty-six years old. I'm your son, not your child. I want to feel your confidence in me. Make me a junior partner. That'll go a long way in my mind."

"You've been thinking this over."

Mitch nodded. Not for the whole time he was in Argentina, but the past six months anyway. "I have ambition, just like you. I know you're still a young man, and you won't be retiring anytime soon. Let me grow into the job that I'll have one day."

"Your behavior recently doesn't give me a lot of faith, much as I hate to say it, Mitch. I've been very disappointed. You don't seem to have the heart for this business that I thought you did. Or the common sense."

Fury sped through Mitch before he controlled it, knowing that was how his father saw it. "You're wrong. Let me prove it."

His father looked away. Mitch knew that expression, the one that said he was debating.

"Okay, son. Here's how. You've made a connection with Annie Barnard, one I sure haven't been able to make. She's got a helluva defensive wall built around her. I want you to stay on with her a while longer. She can't possibly survive the winter. I want that property when she gives up."

"Why?"

"Down the road, I could turn a nice profit with that piece of land."

"By selling it to Morgan," Mitch stated flatly.

"Of course. That's how it's been done between the Ryders and the Morgans for a century and a half. Why would it change now?"

"I won't sabotage her. She doesn't deserve that."

"I'm not saying you should make her fail. You'd just give me a heads-up before Morgan hears about it."

The only thing Mitch knew for sure was that he wasn't ready to leave Annie's place, not if he could help her in some way.

"Look, son, a lot has happened here while you were gone. Profits are down. The biomedical sales have become a gravy train for a lot of ranchers now, not just a few, so that train has left the station for us. We need to make money where we can. And frankly, Mitch, you owe this family something for taking over for you while you licked your wounds."

"Is that what you call grieving for my grandfather? Your father? Licking my wounds?" Mitch came toe-to-toe with him. "I said I know you love me, but you rarely show it, and it's not unconditional, like Granddad's was."

"I know you got your back up when I explained how you weren't doin' things the right way."

"Explained? You *criticized.* A lot. Especially if I suggested any change in how we did things. We should've gone solar years ago. That's a hedge, financially, but you said no. Then when I told you I was getting a divorce, you criticized me even more." Memories came back hard and clear and painful. He'd so badly wanted his father's support during the worst time in his life. "I should make it work, you said. I shouldn't let a mere woman have dominance over me. I guess I was supposed to live unhappily because you don't believe in divorce."

Mitch threw up his hands. "Hell, Dad, *I* don't believe

in divorce. Does anyone? Sometimes a marriage needs to end, period. And I paid for that one for a long time. I learned my lesson. Don't trust any woman. Are you glad I learned that?"

Mitch shoved his fingers through his hair and blew out a long breath.

"We learn most things the hard way, son."

Mitch didn't hear either an apology or any emotion in the tone of voice. Mitch had been right. He wasn't ready to come home, to work for his father again, but he also didn't want family doors shut in his face. This ranch was his home, his future. He and his father had to figure out a way to accomplish that so that they both were happy.

"I'll stay on at Annie's, Dad, not to be your snitch but because I did learn something important from you—how to be a good neighbor, and that I owe my fellow man—or woman—help if I can give it. I can give it to Annie. You want her to fail. I want her to succeed. That's the difference between us."

"You fallin' for this woman?"

"I admire her."

His father's gaze sharpened, as if seeing right through Mitch's spoken motives to the base attraction for the strong, sexy woman trying to make it on her own.

"You have my permission," Jim said.

Mitch wasn't asking for permission. He would've stayed at Annie's without it, but he didn't debate the point. Staying with her suited his purpose, no matter what drove it.

His mother returned, carrying a cardboard box. "Thought you might like to take some beef with you. Adam and Brody were told last night to clean up your house, in case you were moving back home today, but I'm not really sure what you'll find when you get there."

Mitch could only guess. "I won't be moving home, Mom. I'll come back soon, but I've got things to do first." He gave her a hug then used his most charming voice, trying to settle her disappointment that he wasn't staying. "But I've been hankering for a Ryder T-bone."

She shoved him playfully. "Take it with you to the Barnard place, then. There's a rib roast, too, and some fillets."

"Hamburger?" he asked hopefully. "Boys love hamburgers." Big boys and little ones. And maybe one red-blooded woman, too.

Dori opened her refrigerator, added a package from her own stock to the box, then tossed in a few ice packs. Mitch kissed her cheek.

"Thanks, Mom. You're the best."

"Don't be a stranger."

"I promise." He turned to his father and held out his hand. "I'm gonna take Buckshot for a ride before I go. I hope he remembers me."

"Everyone's taken turns exercising him, but I have no doubt he'll be glad to see you. Stay in touch, okay?"

"No cell coverage at The Barn Yard, but I'll email."

The front screen creaked open. "Grammie, I'm here!"

Six-year-old Cassidy Ryder came racing into the kitchen then stopped in her tracks, her corkscrew curls bouncing hard. "Who are you?"

"I'm your uncle Mitch. You haven't seen me in a long time."

"Should I give you a hug?"

Mitch swallowed at the tiny girl's instant acceptance. "I would like that." He hunkered down. She smacked a noisy kiss on his cheek then gave him a hug. When he stood, he was eye to eye with his older brother, Vaughn.

"You've gotten a little gray at the temples since I left," Mitch said, hugging him.

"It'll happen to you, too. Soon I imagine." He pretended to punch his kid brother in the gut. "I didn't see your truck."

"It's in need of repair. I've got parts on order. Dad'll fill you in on the rest."

"Got time to hang out for a while?" Vaughn asked.

"Not at the moment, but how about Monday afternoon?" Annie and Austin would be at the farmer's market. "If my parts come in."

"That'd be good. Mom, will you—"

"We'd be happy to keep our sweetheart. She can stay overnight, too."

"Yay!" Cassidy yelled.

"Come to my house," Vaughn said. "We'll figure out a plan from there."

Mitch felt overwhelmed suddenly and needed to leave. He made quick goodbyes, then headed for the stable, storing his box of beef in the stable refrigerator. The comforting scent of horse, hay and leather greeted him.

"Hey, Buckshot. Hey, boy," Mitch said as he approached the stall. He'd owned the bay gelding for five years before he left, long enough to have a solid relationship.

The horse whinnied and snorted, the white blaze down his face in stark contrast with his black mane. He came forward and nudged Mitch in welcome. A lump formed in his throat as Buckshot continued to rub his face to Mitch's. "Wanna go for a ride?"

Buckshot danced. Mitch found his gear right where he'd left it. He saddled his horse, mounted and took off, trotting out of the stable then letting loose the minute they were outside. Mitch bent over his neck and let him have his head.

Ahh, he'd missed this. He'd ridden every day in Argentina, but it wasn't Buckshot, whom he'd raised and trained from a colt. Nor had it been a free run like this, but a job he did.

Mitch let him set the pace as they explored the ranch. Cattle grazed peacefully, hawks flew overhead, a variety of animals leaped in front and to the side of him. Without conscious thought, he'd been heading for the family cemetery.

The old, hallowed grounds had always been a place of contemplation for Mitch. Often he would conjure up images of his ancestors, remembering stories he'd heard all his life about the outlaw days of the gold rush era. He moved from headstone to headstone, imagining their lives, until he reached his grandfather's, next to his wife, who had died seven years before him, leaving him lost and even more crotchety.

Mitch knelt, tending to the site, pulling a few stray weeds, rearranging the rocks to make a frame around it.

"I miss you, Granddad, more'n I can say."

He climbed aboard Buckshot then took a more meandering path, ending up at his own house, the one he'd built right after he and Marissa had gotten married, a ranch-style structure with four bedrooms, a huge stone fireplace, and a modern kitchen. At least it had been modern when it was built. Maybe it was dated now.

He dismounted, left Buckshot at the railing and climbed the porch stairs. The house wasn't locked. He hadn't expected it to be.

He opened the door and stepped inside then came to a halt. If Adam and Brody had cleaned up the place, he couldn't imagine how bad it had been to start with. Not that things were broken, but it was messy. The kitchen sink was piled high. The trash can was full. The floor hadn't been swept in who knew how long.

He went room to room. The master bedroom looked the same as when he left it, but the attached bathroom… wasn't. He recalled how meticulously Marissa kept the house. She'd hated the dust and dirt that came in with the wind, could never get it vacuumed up or dusted away fast enough. And she let him know about it.

He'd built that house for her—for them. For their future. She'd hated it. And him, apparently. Their marriage lasted about a year, but it hadn't been good after the two-month mark when she started asserting—finally— what she expected, and it wasn't kids or living on this ranch. In the five years they'd dated, she'd never uttered a word about either.

Mitch closed his eyes, trying to regain his mood from his ride. He was born on this land, would probably die on this land. He wasn't going to let a few bad memories steal his joy.

He left his brothers a note, not criticizing their housekeeping skills but saying he'd catch up with them soon. He was looking forward to seeing them, and his sister Haley, although he'd have to drive into town to catch up with her. She hadn't built on her property, either, but had a small house in town, walking distance to her work at the rehab hospital.

Mitch and Buckshot made their way back to the main stable. A ranch hand Mitch didn't know offered to take care of the horse, and Mitch accepted, wanting to get home before Annie worried that he'd left with her truck.

Home. He couldn't think of it that way. It was her home, not his. He'd just been in his home, and before that the house where he'd grown up. That was still home, too.

The twenty miles of highway back to The Barn Yard felt like two hundred as he contemplated his next move. He should tell her his last name, convince her he was staying to help her succeed. Would she believe him or send him on his way? Then what would she do?

Maybe she could get past learning the truth, but she was justifiably protective of Austin. She wouldn't see Mitch as a good influence, but someone who'd lied. She'd talked about the Ryder family with him. He'd been in his bedroom listening when his father and brother had come with their proposition. She'd confided in Mitch, telling him things she wouldn't want his family to know.

He was stuck between being honest with her and earning back his position with his father at the family ranch.

He blocked the debate in his head as he neared her farm, noticing the sign they'd hung, big and bright, hard to miss. It needed something else, something decorative and representative, like chickens or berries. His mother would know. She was the artist in the family—and his sister Jenny, too, but she was at college.

Bo barked, running alongside the truck as Mitch pulled in. Austin was grinning ear to ear. Mitch'd been gone four hours. It felt like an entirely different world from this one. Prosperity versus struggle. Large, boisterous family versus mother and son. Success versus hope. Such incredible hope.

Annie came out of the high tunnel, a soft, welcoming smile on her face. Her hands and arms were covered with dirt. He wanted to give her a proper hello, a hug and kiss, but that was impossible. Even if Austin hadn't been home, Mitch couldn't do that. He had no right.

He jumped down from the truck, pulling the cardboard box across the seat, then presenting it to Annie. The packages were labeled. Her eyes lit up.

"Do you know how to barbecue?" she asked.

"Are ranchers stubborn?" he asked rhetorically.

"We will feast tonight," she said, then hesitated. "You're working mostly for room and board. You shouldn't be spending your money on food for us."

"I traded a little work for it." It was a small lie, one to make her accept the gift. And damn, but he wanted a steak for dinner.

"Have you eaten lunch?" she asked.

His stomach would have rejected anything until now. "No. But I can throw together some PB and J. I don't need much."

He stashed the meat in the refrigerator then made himself at home in her kitchen, the first time she hadn't fixed his meal. He paid attention to the room now, having his mother's kitchen and even his own to compare it with. She didn't own a dishwasher, and no appliance was newer than twenty years. Every surface was spotless, but wear and tear showed in chips in the Formica countertop and cabinets that hadn't seen fresh paint in a long time. She'd made bright yellow curtains, however, and a matching apron that hung from a hook, providing a splash of color.

And she loved it. Wanted to stay.

"Mitch! Mitch! Come quick!" Austin hollered.

He raced out of the house, looked around frantically.

"Over here. Mom's stuck."

Visions of Annie buried under timber filled his head, then he rounded the corner behind the high tunnel and saw Annie looking embarrassed and chagrined, and definitely stuck—in a mud hole.

"What did you do?" he asked, trying not to laugh,

while Austin had lost that ability already. He was laughing his head off.

She lifted her chin. "I left the hose running in the pile of new dirt—since before you left, I might add. The dirt wasn't packed, and I didn't think about that. I went to walk over it to turn off the hose and it grabbed me like quicksand. Would you quit laughing and help get me out of here?"

"Yes, to the latter, but no to the former." He chuckled as he went behind her and hooked his forearms under her and pulled. There was no way around it—his arms pressed against her breasts. It was the only way he could get enough leverage to loosen her.

"Austin, start scraping the mud from her legs with your hands. See if you can dig a trench to her feet."

After a minute a sucking sound filled the air and her legs popped free, although her shoes were left behind.

"Mom!" Austin said in mock horror. "Say excuse me."

Annie threw a handful of mud at him. He threw some back. Pretty soon they were all slinging mud at each other, some landing in clumps on Bo as well, who happily played along.

Finally they all collapsed, panting hard.

Annie's chest heaved. Mitch pretended to block the sun with his hand so that he could get an eyeful without Austin noticing.

"Welcome home," Annie said pertly.

There it was. She used the word *home,* too. He decided not to make a big deal of it. "Thanks. What do you say we take Austin and go for a swim?"

"Where?"

"A place I used to go as a kid."

She looked around. "I don't know. There's so much to do."

"The next two days will be busy harvesting for the farmer's market, right?"

"Yes."

"Then let's play a little today. Pay it forward." He saw more indecision in her pretty green eyes. "I've decided to stay around a little longer, Annie. If you want me to, that is."

"A man who brings his own steak? Yeah, I think I'll keep you."

Her tone was light, but she couldn't hide her relief.

"Then let's go swimming." More than anything, he wanted to see the curvy Ms. Annie Barnard in a bathing suit.

Chapter Nine

"Is that the same rope you used to swing from, Mitch?" Austin asked as he pulled off his sneakers and T-shirt.

"I hope not or it'd be pretty rotten by now." He undressed to his bathing suit, too. "Let me test it first."

Annie took off her shorts, but left her shirt on, as well as her old sneakers, which she intended to keep on, no matter what. She didn't want to step on anything, whether animal, vegetable or mineral.

Mitch was a sight in his trunks. Muscular but not overdone. Just enough dark body hair to make her fingers twitch. And the patience of a saint as he instructed Austin on how to use the rope, when to let go and where to swim from there.

Annie didn't like rivers or cold water. She was also nervous about wearing just a bathing suit in front of Mitch. The only suit she owned was a bikini from before she'd given birth. Before her breasts had come into full bloom, as her mother had called it. Annie had been a little appalled by the sight when she glanced in the mirror. She wasn't falling out of the top, but she filled it to the brim.

The problem was, she *wanted* Mitch to notice, even though it was foolish to do so. Everything about him being there was unreal enough. She'd almost told him she needed to know his last name now that he was going to be around longer, but the kind of otherworldliness of the situation, which she'd been enjoying, stopped her. If she knew his name, everything would become real. She wasn't ready for real.

Mitch yelled like Tarzan as he swung out over the water and dropped, then came up sputtering. "Warm as a hot spring," he said, grinning.

Austin grabbed the rope and followed suit, letting go when Mitch yelled at him to drop.

"Oh, yeah, a hot spring!" Austin shouted when he came to the surface.

"Your lips are already blue," Annie said, settling down on a rock to watch them, her feet dangling in the water. She didn't let them see her react to the cold water.

"It's not that cold, Mom. You get used to it in a hurry."

"Chicken," Mitch said, taunting her, obviously knowing her ego wouldn't allow her to be perceived by her son as being afraid of anything.

"In a while. I just want to bask in the warmth for now." She closed her eyes and leaned back on her hands, her face to the sun, trying to remember the last time they'd done something unrelated to survival. But now that there was an extra person to help, they could plan some fun things to do.

Except Mitch wouldn't want to be in public.

When had her life gotten so complicated?

Well, she knew when. The better question was why? Fate, as Mitch believed? A grand design? To succeed where she might not have otherwise? Or to give up gracefully when—if—the time came rather than cause irreparable damage to her *and* her son? Austin should learn there's a time to cut your losses and still hold your head high.

"Come on, Mom," Austin yelled. "You're missing all the fun."

She glanced at Mitch, who wisely didn't say anything. She couldn't leave her shirt on because she would have to drive home in wet clothes, so she peeled it over her head and tossed it up the slope to where the rest of their clothes were piled.

"Use the rope," Austin said. "Get it over with at once."

"No, thank you." She wasn't a strong swimmer. Easing in would work just fine for her.

She felt the intensity of Mitch's gaze, even as he continued to play with Austin in some kind of cat-and-mouse chase. Then they took turns on the rope, seeing how far into the pool they could land. Inch by inch, Annie entered the cold stream that was in perpetual motion. She was about to finally just duck under and get it over with when she slipped on a slimy rock and tumbled in.

Competent hands grabbed her within seconds, but she'd already gone into full panic mode.

"I've got you," Mitch said calmly. "Just relax. You're safe."

She clung to him, her arms locked around his neck. His hands settled at her waist as their bodies pressed together, gliding slickly.

"I'm going to walk you to the bank, okay," he said,

bending close, adding, "Is it in really poor taste right now to say thank you for wearing that particular bikini?"

She laughed, which was what she was sure he'd intended to happen.

"I only have this one."

"You fill it out nicely."

Her panic left as quickly as it'd come, replaced with awareness of him, especially when he cupped her rear with his hand as he gave her boost out of the water— something she didn't need but was glad he'd done.

"Are you okay, Mom?" Austin had come up beside them.

"I'm fine. It was silly. And, see, that's why your dad and I insisted on swimming lessons for you. I never had them. Keep playing." She wanted Mitch to keep his hands on her and didn't think Austin would care, as if Mitch was comforting her, getting her settled again.

He had her sit on the rock again, warm from the sun, and grabbed a towel to wrap around her, pulled her ponytail outside the fabric, then rubbed her back through it.

"Good?" he asked.

She didn't know how to answer that. Yes, his hands felt good on her, but she had a feeling he was trying to make sure she'd recovered. "Your hands are wonderful," she said, then got nervous she'd said the wrong thing when he paused. "You warmed me up fast."

A long pause ensued. Finally he gave her a look so hot, so direct and so inviting, she couldn't speak. He stood and moved down the banking, keeping his back to Austin. Mitch's wet swim trunks didn't hide anything from her interested eyes. She raised her gaze slowly. When she reached his face, he fell backward into the stream.

Annie blew out a long, shaky breath. She wanted

him. She couldn't have him. Shouldn't, either, considering how little she knew about him. Like where had he gotten the beef? Where had he exchanged work for it, and why wouldn't he tell her?

She shouldn't trust him, and yet she did.

They stayed until Austin couldn't stop shivering. Even then he wanted to keep playing. He was sent to take a hot bath when they got home, while Mitch and Annie made dinner—T-bones, baked potatoes and a fresh green salad.

"That was the best steak I've ever had," Annie said after dinner, not touching her stomach, afraid it would burst.

"You know Mitch brought a whole box full of it, Mom. You didn't have to eat the whole thing at one time."

"Yes, I did. No regrets." She thought Mitch looked happy, too.

"I'm going to go work off dinner," he said after the dishes were done.

"Doing what?"

"Fill the raised beds with some aged potting soil so that you can plant tomorrow." He left without waiting for her response, apparently wanting to get away from her.

Because she tempted him too much? Because he was embarrassed about what had happened and what they'd said at the stream?

He was still outdoors when Austin went to bed and Annie showered. She didn't want to go to bed wondering where things stood with them.

She wrapped her robe over her summer pajamas, tightened the sash and put on her slippers. From a distance she could hear him mumbling in the high tunnel, but she only caught an occasional word: *fate, Grand-dad, self-control.*

When she reached him she laid a hand on his back. He spun toward her and raised his shovel, which he instantly dropped then pulled her into his arms, kissing her with a need that matched her own.

"You smell good," he said against her mouth, then kissed her deeper. "You taste hot and sexy." He pulled her robe aside and curved his hands over her breasts, rubbing the fabric back and forth, abrading her taut flesh, driving her wild. "You feel like my dreams."

He licked at her lips as his thumbs brushed her nipples, then he deepened the kiss with his searching tongue, throaty sounds coming from him. She'd never felt so desired. She slipped her hands under his shirt, flattened them against his skin, feeling his muscles flex as she let her fingertips investigate the planes and angles of his body, the bone structure beneath, the flat belly. He was so hard, where she was so soft.

He was about to lift her pajama top when a sound intruded. Not human, she didn't think, and not a threat, but it brought awareness of standing in the greenhouse. The lights were on in the fading daylight. Anyone outside it would see them, not in detail, but enough to know they were kissing and touching.

As much as she hated to, she backed away, saying nothing, not knowing what to say, and returned to the house. They'd hit a fork in the road of their relationship. For now, they had no options. But when Austin went to see his dad? What then? It was only two weeks from now.

Two whole weeks of tension. And then what?

Maybe he'd even be gone by then and there would be no dilemma.

Annie climbed into bed. She stayed awake until Mitch finally came in and showered. She heard him stop by her bedroom, silently urged him to come inside, then his soft footfalls as he walked away, the click of his bedroom door punctuating the moment.

Case closed. Period. No further discussion or action required.

Mitch was up earlier than usual the next day, having tossed and turned. He got the coffee started then leaned against the counter. He'd lost control last night, and now there was no turning back.

How would she act this morning? Aloof? Overly friendly? Possessive? Why had she left without a word?

If she hadn't left he might have hauled her off to his truck and made love to her. He kept a couple of blankets in the backseat. No one would've caught them. They could've satisfied their curiosity about each other and been done with it. Now it was only going to build until he either would have to leave or they had to sleep together. He didn't see any other options.

"Good morning," she said from behind him in her usual cheery morning voice. "How'd you sleep?"

She asked him that every day, but today felt different.

"I tossed a lot," he said, facing her. She was already dressed, which was unusual. Generally she wore her robe the first half hour, through the first cup of coffee. "How about you?"

"The same." She remained cheerful. "So, today we'll pick flowers, make bouquets and store them in buckets of water. I'd also like to get the lettuces planted in the first few raised boxes."

He tried to figure her out. Were they just going forward as if nothing had happened?

Well, okay. He would take her lead and go with it. It made sense, anyway. He'd intended to make his grandfather proud by keeping complete control of himself, having sat through many lectures on the subject of respecting women. He hadn't kept *complete* control, but she'd given him a second chance now by pretending it had never happened.

"You're the boss," he said, creating an even bigger space between them, also a good thing, he figured. "How much do you take to market?"

"Twenty mixed bouquets and ten of single varieties. A restaurant owner bought several of those last week. She prefers her tables have only one kind of bloom. She said it adds to the level of sophistication. That was great information to know. She also told me she'd be back this week. It's regulars like that who'll matter most in the long run."

"Which produce will you take?"

"The strawberries that won't last until the weekend U-pick. Pickling cukes, lettuce, potatoes. It'll be more than I figure I can sell because I trade with other growers. My lettuce will be a big draw."

"When does the market stop operating for the year?"

"Mid-October. But I'm going to have the pumpkin patch. And I'll sell fall flowers at the same time. Maybe pies, too."

He couldn't imagine her doing more than breaking even on her expenses.

She came close to him and set her hand on his arm for a moment. "I know what you're thinking. But I can't give up yet."

"I wasn't thinking that. I was considering what else would sell over the winter."

"As soon as all the harvest is done, I'm going to start

calling on stores and restaurants. I have to have enough product to offer a certain amount every week. If I can get that going, I can make a living." She walked past him. "However, I can't make it by selling only locally. I have to expand, even if it means driving to San Francisco once a week."

"You've done your research."

"And I'm being realistic."

He could see that. Every day he admired her more.

"I'm going to get started clipping flowers," she said. "They're best early in the day."

"What can I do?"

"There are a bunch of five-gallon buckets in the barn. If you could fill them about one-third with water and bring them out to the garden, that would be great."

They worked until Austin joined them, stopped for breakfast, then finished up by noon. Mitch could cut flowers, strip leaves and pluck off wilted petals, but he couldn't arrange them artfully.

"Can we go swimming again?" Austin asked during lunch.

"Not today," Annie said. She'd put a pot of chili on the stove early that morning, adding hamburger to it for the first time in ages, giving the dish a different taste.

"You know, Mom, Sunday's supposed to be a day of rest."

Mitch laughed, realized Annie didn't think it was funny and dug into his chili with more gusto than previously.

"Yes, Austin, I've heard that. Unfortunately, it isn't always possible."

"But we're done working for today."

"We're done with the flowers. We need to get the plantings in the high tunnel done."

"It's not fair. None of my friends have to work all the time." He shoved away from the table and ran down the hall, not quite slamming his bedroom door.

She stared after him. Mitch hadn't been in her situation, but he understood how hard it must be.

"Maybe while I'm here he could do a little less," he said.

"And when you leave it'll be that much harder for him to readjust to his chores again. He and I have discussed this a lot. I wish he didn't have to work so hard, but we don't have any choice. I thought he understood."

"Of course he does. He's got a good head on his shoulders, but play is also a kid's work, you know? They learn a lot through the games and sports they play. We touched on this before."

"Yes, although from what you said, you spent most of your time working."

"Which is why I identify with Austin. One of the reasons I started to play football was to have a reason to get out of some of the chores, then I fell in love with the game. After I could drive, I had more freedom to do things in the evening. But I still had to be up at five to do morning chores."

"What he's asking for involves *me,* though," she said. "He can't just walk across the street and ask a kid to come play. He needs to be driven to town, or have someone driven here."

"What he's asking for today is to go swimming. That's all you're dealing with. There aren't a whole lot of days left to do that," he said idly. "I could take him, and you could have a little alone time. Bet you don't get much of that."

She compressed her lips for a moment. "Almost none."

Mitch said nothing. He understood why she worked Austin as hard as she did. He just didn't believe Austin needed to at the moment.

"You really would take him swimming?"

"Your son is good company, Annie."

She sat back, looking bemused. "Alone time. I'm not sure what I would do."

"Well, I figured you'd be planting your lettuce, like you told Austin."

Her cheeks flushed a little.

He patted her hand. "It's all right. I won't tell a soul that you want some playtime, too."

"You *have* lightened the load around here."

"Then don't be gettin' after yourself for taking a couple of hours just for you. We can all plant the lettuce in a few hours. There's time for both."

Austin's bedroom door opened. He scuffed his feet as he came down the hall and into the dining room. "I'm sorry, Mom. I didn't mean to be selfish."

"It's all right, honey. I've thought it over, and decided we really do have a little extra time these days because of Mitch. So, yes, you can go swimming. Mitch said he'd take you."

He grinned. "Thanks!"

"Got a fishing pole?" Mitch asked.

"Do we, Mom?"

"Not that I'm aware of. And no licenses," Annie added pointedly.

"He doesn't need one, not until he's sixteen. I'll see if I can borrow some equipment and show him how to use it another day. That swimming hole used to have plenty of trout."

A few minutes later they loaded towels, a thermos of ice water and snacks into the truck and took off. Annie watched until they were out of sight, holding Bo's collar so he wouldn't chase after them. Bo howled a couple of times, feeling left out, then he went after a chicken and forgot his boy was gone, at least for the moment.

"What should I do?" Annie asked Bo when he returned to her side. She got a cocked-head, ears-pricked answer in return. It wasn't as if she'd never been alone at the farm. During the school year she was alone all day.

What were her options? Work in the greenhouse. Make a blueberry pie. Take a bubble bath…which seemed way too indulgent on a Sunday afternoon, but was the most tempting of her choices. That and reading a good book at the same time. Heaven.

Before she could decide, she heard a vehicle coming up her driveway. She hoped it wasn't one of the Ryder or Morgan men. She wanted to enjoy her time alone.

But it was Marissa Mazur. Alone.

Chapter Ten

"I'm so sorry for not calling first," Marissa said as she got out of her car. "I just took a chance you'd be home."

As usual her hair and makeup were perfect. She wore jeans and a long blouse, but Annie noted the small bump formed by the lives growing inside her. "How're you feeling?"

"Morning sickness every day. Ugh. It should end soon, though. I've just started my second trimester. Your place is looking really good."

"Thanks. I hired some help to get it to a point I can keep up. It's been a huge relief." Annie was torn about inviting her inside. She didn't really want to develop a friendship with the ex-wife of the man Annie desired. "Would you like some iced tea?" she asked, not wanting to seem antisocial. Marissa had been kind to Austin.

"I would love some, thanks. I've been running errands for hours. Or maybe just one hour. But it seems like six." She smiled so engagingly that Annie could picture Mitch being drawn to her.

"Why don't you take a seat on the porch. I'll be right back."

Annie added a couple of blueberry muffins to the tray she carried out and set on the low table in front of the glider. Marissa sat in the rocker, but wasn't rocking it.

"Motion sickness, too," she said, a hand over her abdomen as she accepted the glass of tea and muffin. "I can't believe I'm thirty-five years old and still having babies. There was a time I never wanted any. Ever. Now I'll have five. Sure shows you how time can change things. Or the right man," she added thoughtfully.

Annie felt stuck. It would be natural to ask questions about her comments, but did she want the answers? And if Marissa discovered Mitch was working for her, and living with her, would she feel deceived?

"I guess we all kiss a few frogs before our prince comes along," Annie said. "So, what brings you here today?" she asked, changing the subject.

"Flowers. I know you've been selling them at the farmer's market, and I can't get there tomorrow night. I was hoping to buy some from you today."

"Of course. We picked this morning. You can have your choice."

"Thanks." Marissa was quiet for a moment then sighed. "That's not the whole truth, Annie. I'm lonely. I grew up here, but I moved away years ago. We just came back last year. It's been hard finding girlfriends. A lot of people carry a grudge for the way I treated my ex-husband. I liked you the minute I met you. I think we have a lot in common."

If you only knew. Annie was hungry for girlfriends,

too, and under other circumstances would've made the return effort. Now she was stuck.

"You're not saying anything," Marissa said quietly. She set her tea glass on the small table next to the rocker then stood. "Maybe my reputation preceded me. I apologize for taking your time."

Annie couldn't let her go thinking the worst. "Please don't leave. Honestly, I hadn't heard anything about you, good or bad, since we met. I just have such limited time available. I hope that will change."

After a few seconds, Marissa sat. "I'm supersensitive these days. Hormones, you know."

Annie laughed. "I remember. PMS on steroids."

"Exactly!"

Annie led the discussion into neutral territory—their children. They passed the better part of a half hour comparing notes about kids, sharing recipes and life in the Red Valley. Then Marissa chose a mixed bouquet and left. By then, enough time had passed that Annie decided not to loll in a bubble bath. Instead she started on the lettuce planting. She'd tilled in compost a week ago in preparation. Growing it in the high tunnel would be a different experience from the in-the-ground crops she'd grown previously, but their short growth life would give her answers about success or failure quickly, as well as the different varieties she was trying. She would plant garlic between the rows to help control aphids, and then seed new rows every couple of weeks, rotating her crop.

Annie found herself humming as she worked, anticipating Mitch and Austin coming home, thoroughly enjoying planting. The task soothed her, but she decided she was also feeling more confident about her future success than a week ago. What she needed was an online presence. A website where local restaurants could find her specialty products. She wondered how expensive it would be to have a site created.

She heard her truck coming up the driveway and walked over to greet Mitch and Austin. Bo was running alongside and barking. Austin hopped out of the truck and raced to Annie, hugging her hard.

"My Popsicle boy," she said, wrapping him tight. "Did you have fun?"

"Yes!" He wriggled free. "I know. I know. Take a hot shower." He grinned then ran off, taking the stairs in almost one leap.

"He's fearless," Mitch said, coming up more slowly.

"Is that a good thing?"

"It can be."

The vague answer made her smile and shake her head. "Are you a Popsicle, too?"

"I could use a warm-up hug."

She didn't know what to say. She wouldn't mind it herself, especially since skin to skin was the best way to deal with a cold body.

"I'm kidding," he said, cupping her arm for just a moment. "Sort of."

She just stared at him, wishing for the same thing, knowing it was impossible.

"Did you enjoy your free time? Looks like you were working."

"Not the whole time, just the past half hour or so. Before that I had company."

They walked up the porch steps. She indicated he should sit on the glider, because the sun was hitting it.

"Marissa dropped by. It was pretty uncomfortable."

"What did she want?"

"A bouquet. She said she couldn't make it to the market tomorrow night."

"And?"

"She's looking to be friends."

"Is that something you would like?"

"Frankly, yes. I like her."

"I'm sorry I've complicated your life." Mitch leaned forward, his arms on his thighs. "I can leave now, Annie, and you could be friends with her. She wouldn't know I'd ever been here."

"Austin knows. Your name is bound to come up at some point."

"I'm sorry," he said again, meaning it. He'd lived in the same place most of his life and had lifelong friends, plus his siblings, who were close. She'd moved around a lot and wanted very much to establish a community for herself.

"I didn't learn anything new about you," Annie said, "except that she was the villain in your divorce."

"It wasn't pretty." Mitch looked away. He didn't want to go there. "You worked on the lettuce."

She rocked slowly, looking serene. "I found it soothing. Even Bo just curled up and slept most of the time. I do love digging in my dirt, and I especially like seeing little green shoots come up. I've come to realize that I made a mistake early on by trying to grow too many different kinds of produce. Specializing is the way to go. Fewer chances of messing up."

"So that means what?"

"Flowers, berries, specialty potatoes and lettuces, which can be year-round. I'll grow enough tomatoes for my own use, pumpkins for the Halloween traffic, but that's it. It finally makes sense to me."

It made sense to Mitch, too, even without knowing her business. In his line of work, specializing also made sense, although when his father had branched out into the biomedical supply field, it had increased their cash flow enormously. But now that part of the business had apparently flattened out. They needed to come up with other ways to bring in income.

Mitch had ideas, especially regarding solar power. He'd had plenty of time to think while he was gone. Now to convince his father to implement them.

Austin came bounding out of the house and plopped down next to Mitch on the glider. "We saw tons of trout, Mom. We're gonna catch dinner the next time we go."

"Will you eat it? If not, you need to catch and release."

"Do you like trout, Mitch?" Austin asked.

"Love it, especially cooked in foil on the barbecue."

"Then I will, too."

Mitch saw a frown settle on Annie's face. Because Austin was too obviously attached? That worried Mitch more than Marissa finding out he was living at Annie's place. The boy had been hurt enough by his father. Mitch didn't want to add to it.

"Mitch," Annie said, "if you can give me a list of what you would need for the roof repair on the barn, I could go into town early tomorrow and pick up the supplies before the farmer's market starts."

He'd blocked it from his mind. Every day he'd looked at the to-do list he'd created the first morning, checking off items as he went, ignoring the roof. "I'm not even sure. You might just go to the building supply store and tell them the problem and let them show you what you need. Is there more than the one big leak in the corner?"

"There are a couple others," she said apologetically. "Nothing major, just drips."

"Then you should probably get some product that seals small holes, too." Great. Not only would he have to climb the ladder but he'd have to get on the roof itself and inspect it for other leaks. He really wished she could afford to hire a roofer.

"What do you say? Shall we get some work done?" he asked, standing. He'd enjoyed the day of fun, but he knew Annie felt a need to keep working.

"I got all the lettuce planted," Annie said. "At least for now. Every couple of weeks I'll plant more so there's a fresh supply. It's going to be great using the bedding boxes. No more bending over." She stood. "How about we have a new tradition for as long as you're here—no work on Sunday. Well, except to pick and prep the flowers. Can't escape that."

"Yay!" Austin jumped up. "Does that mean I can play video games?"

"You can do whatever you want."

"Cool!" Off he went, the screen door slamming behind him.

"What are your plans?" Mitch asked.

"I'm going to bake a blueberry pie. How about you?"

His first choice would be to take her bed for the rest of the afternoon. "If you don't mind loaning me your truck, I'd like to go do something. The parts should arrive for my truck tomorrow, and I won't have to ask again."

"Sure. Will you be home for dinner?"

"Six o'clock?"

"Okay. Have fun."

He hadn't returned her keys yet, so he dug them out of his pocket. He wanted to kiss her goodbye something fierce. He continued to stare at her.

She cocked her head. "What?"

Austin was close enough to hear their conversation if he was paying attention, so Mitch came up close to

Annie, watching her stiffen the nearer he got. "You're a helluva woman, Annie Barnard."

Her eyebrows arched. "I am?"

"You're proving to be a lot more adaptable than I expected. You've lightened up considerably."

"I haven't been under the same degree of stress. Because of you."

It must have cost her a lot to tell him that, to show some vulnerability, because she was one of the proudest women he'd ever met. "I'm glad I could help."

He ran a hand down her arm to her hand and squeezed it, then he jogged to the truck and took himself off to Ryder Ranch. It was easier coming home this time. His gut clenched a little, but not like before. There was usually a family barbecue on Sunday afternoons, but maybe not, now that all of his siblings were adults with lives of their own. All he wanted was to take a ride. If he could avoid his parents this time around, that was fine with him.

But it wasn't meant to be. Various four-wheelers and trucks were parked near the house. His brothers Adam and Brody were out front tossing a football. Ranch hands and their families were milling about, children chasing children, and dogs barking, playing along.

Adam spotted him and waved. Mitch stopped but didn't turn off the engine. Brody came, too, as Adam approached the truck. The Ryder family connection was strong among the four brothers, their coloring and physique similar, but their personalities far different from each other.

"Welcome home." Brody, the youngest of the brothers at twenty-six, hopped up on the running board, grinning. Adam, twenty-nine, pounded Mitch's back. "You come for dinner? Mom was hopin'."

"I came to take Buckshot for a ride." And himself. "I wanted to talk to you both, though. I take it Mom and Dad clued you in about where I've been living lately."

"Yep," Adam said. "I've seen the lady myself at the farmer's market. I'd hang around her place, too, if I could."

"Knock it off."

"Touchy, touchy. So. Are you kicking Adam and me out of your house?"

"Not yet, but I need a favor. I figure you've been living rent-free for three years, you owe me a few."

"Like hell we have," Brody said. "We've been paying rent all along. Dad didn't send it to you?"

Mitch shook his head.

"Anyway, we're brothers. We do favors for each other. What do you need?" Adam asked.

"You know I have a little problem with heights."

"A little problem? Hell. That's like saying Winkle was sweet and gentle."

Mitch laughed. That big old bull had hated everyone, but especially their granddad. The two had legendary staring contests.

"Um, Annie's barn's got a little hole in the roof. How about you come out a week from tomorrow during the farmer's market when she'll be gone? We'll get it fixed for her."

"Isn't that the place that Dad says is gonna go under before the year's up?"

Mitch clenched his teeth. "I'm asking a favor. Yes or no?"

"Course we will. Hey, sorry for the mess at the house yesterday. We didn't have time to clean up."

"It's okay. Actually, I'm glad someone's been living

in it. How come you haven't built your houses on your own properties yet?"

"Didn't seem to be a need to," Adam said. "Maybe you comin' home's lit a fire for us, though."

Brody shrugged. "I figure I'll wait until I've got a bride to bring to it. Let her take part in the decision." He clamped his mouth shut for a few seconds. "Sorry, Mitch. I know you did that for Marissa."

"I got the house I wanted. Did you know she's back in the valley?"

"Yeah. Saw her a couple of times. Don't think she saw me, though," Brody said. "She had kids with her."

"She's got three, with twins on the way."

All three brothers went silent at that.

"Didn't know a leopard could change its spots like that," Adam said. "Sorry, bro."

"I'm over it. Her. All of it. Have been for years. Listen, I'm gonna go saddle up."

"You don't want to say hi to Mom?"

"I'd end up staying for hours, and you know it. Tell her I'll catch her one day this week. It's good to see you both. I've missed you."

His brothers moved back. He waved out the window as he took off.

Mitch took Buckshot in a different direction from yesterday, a place with fewer emotional ties, just open grazing land, fallow for now. He gave the horse his head, and they rode as one. There was little in the world that felt as good.

Except maybe a warm, willing woman in his arms—although not just any woman.

He led Buckshot back to the stable more slowly. Mitch wasn't soothed by the ride as much as he'd hoped. Thoughts swirled in his head, truths and lies, hopes and disappointments. He hadn't focused on the future for a long time, just the past and present. He'd kept his mind as blank as possible while he was in Argentina, doing his job day to day, not planning anything.

Until the past few months. He'd finally come home when his father ordered him for the fourth time because he was ready to come back.

When he rode into the yard and dismounted, his father came out from the stable to greet him.

"You can't at least say hello to your mother?" he asked.

"I told Annie I'd have her truck back. I saw Mom yesterday, Dad. I'll come visit soon." He walked Buckshot inside, was officially introduced to the new hand who'd taken care of his horse the day before and left his horse with him. He would've groomed Buckshot himself except he figured his father would hang around the whole time. They walked toward Annie's truck.

"Everything going okay?"

"Nothing's changed since yesterday." Mitch eyed his father. "Adam and Brody said they've been paying rent on my house."

"The money's tucked away in a brokerage account Vaughn chose. He says you've made some gains on it, but you'll have to ask him. I stayed out of the decisions. Figured you wouldn't want me involved."

Mitch was a good saver and spent little, anyway, but to find he had a cushion made him relax in a big way. "Thanks."

"Thank your mother. It was her idea." They reached the truck. "Don't be a stranger."

Mitch nodded then climbed into the truck. He started the engine, put it in Reverse.

"Son."

He looked at his father, saw an expression he couldn't interpret. "What?"

"He wouldn't want you to keep on grieving."

Mitch clenched his fists. "I know."

He kicked up dust as he drove the long road out of the ranch. When he reached the highway, he turned in the direction of Annie's place and gave it some gas. He didn't slow down, not until he'd gone ten miles past The Barn Yard. He pulled over under some trees and rested his forehead against the steering wheel.

His father was right. He should just remember all the good times, something that might be easier if Mitch hadn't begged his grandfather to hold on longer than he should have. Because Mitch couldn't bear to lose him, he caused his grandfather a great deal of pain in the end.

For that, Mitch would never forgive himself.

Chapter Eleven

Late the next morning, Annie approached the shed where Austin and Mitch were installing the new parts in his truck. She could hear Mitch describing what the part was, what it did, where it fit and what connected to it. They'd already picked all the produce for the farmer's market, then loaded it and the buckets of flowers plus her booth setup parts in her truck, which was parked in the shade. They would leave right after lunch.

She wished Mitch would come with her but knew he wouldn't. He'd been in a strange mood since returning yesterday—quiet and distant. She wondered where he'd gone. The same place as the day before?

To see a woman, maybe? That possibility didn't seem likely, considering his obvious attraction to her, but then, she barely knew him. Anything was possible.

"How's it going?" she asked.

"We'll find out soon," Mitch said, straightening and

wiping his hands with a rag. "I could end up replacing every part, one by one, until I've got it fixed, I suppose."

"Lunch is ready. Can you stop?"

"I'd rather keep working. And I'm not really hungry yet."

He'd barely touched his breakfast, which was totally unlike him. He and Austin usually consumed hearty amounts.

"What time do you think you'll be home?" he asked.

"The market's open from three to seven, then we have to take down our canopy and stow the booth. Sometime around eight, depending on how much we all talk after. There's chili in the fridge you can heat up, if you want. I'll wrap your sandwich up now and put it in there, too."

"Thanks." He stuck his head back under the hood.

"Can I eat my sandwich while we're driving?" Austin asked. "I want to keep helping Mitch."

"Sure."

Half an hour later, Annie and Austin headed for town, first to the building supply store then to set up their site. It wasn't a big marketplace. Only about fifteen people set up booths on a regular basis, but it was in a good location with lots of traffic and easy parking nearby. One of the biggest draws was the barbecued sausage sandwich booth, which moved each week according to which way the wind blew. Many residents came just for that, then ended up buying homemade beef jerky or table flowers or farm-fresh eggs. Local musicians took turns on a nearby corner.

Annie and Austin set up their pop-up canopy in minutes, then hung their sign from the back. They put three tables in a U-shape, where they placed a bushel of two varieties of baby potatoes, a bunch of pickling cucumbers and an ice chest filled with baby lettuces. The buckets of bouquets sat on the ground beneath the tables, except for a couple placed on the tables. Annie wore a cash apron with plenty of change.

Early birds usually showed up for first selections, and today was no different, including the organic restaurant owner, Brenna James, who'd become a regular already.

"Hey, Annie, how's it going?" Brenna asked. The petite brunette with shiny long hair and near-black eyes shook hands. Annie figured she was in her forties.

"Very well, thanks. I've got two choices for you this time—dahlias and asters. Neither has much scent, so they'd work well for your tables."

"Oh, I love the dahlias! What glorious colors, and they're so big. They really make a statement. I'll take three bundles." She glanced at the bushel of potatoes. "These are gorgeous little fingerlings. I'll take a few pounds. A mix of the colors, please."

Annie could hardly contain her excitement as people around them listened in. Everyone knew Brenna was particular.

"May I?" Brenna said, plucking a leaf of baby red leaf lettuce from the cooler.

"Of course."

Brenna pronounced it wonderful and asked for two plastic bags full. "Do you grow shallots?"

"I haven't, but I can look into doing that. I'm pretty sure they have a year-round growing season."

"A shallot vinaigrette would be perfect with these greens. I need to come out to your farm and see what you've got. Do you have official organic status yet?"

"I've submitted the paperwork." *Two days ago, after getting the high tunnel up and running.* She gave Brenna her business card. "I'm just waiting for the inspection. But I've complied with everything required to pass. Feel free to come by. Austin, please give Ms. James one of your flyers. Maybe Saturday would work for you, and you could choose some berries, too."

"Sounds good, thanks." She paid for her purchases and moved on to Ginny Otta's booth, where the scent of peaches was heady.

And so it begins, Annie thought as she gave another customer a flyer about the U-pick coming up.

"You're starting out well," Ginny said after completing her transaction with Brenna. Ginny owned and operated a substantial organic orchard plus was director of the farmer's market. Fiftyish, honey-blond and vivacious, she lit up the market with her friendliness. She was also the most knowledgeable grower Annie knew, and she'd been generous with her advice. The farmer's market was her pet project, something she did for the community, as she otherwise direct-marketed almost all her produce to San Francisco and southern Oregon outlets. She was Annie's hero.

"It's exciting," Annie said. "Every week I sell more. I'm so hopeful, Ginny, especially now that I've got the high tunnel up and operating. Thank you so much for recommending the handyman. He's been incredible."

"Really?" Ginny's brows went up. "I heard he took one look at the place and left, scared of all the work."

"How strange. Well, I guess he changed his mind. He did show up a day late, so he must have thought it over. I'm telling you, he's been fabulous. He's up before I am, and works really hard, plus he's been good for Austin. I feel lucky he came back to—"

A customer hailed Ginny to purchase peaches, then suddenly customers appeared at almost every stall, old friends gathering, products being tasted, everyone catching up on the town news. With a trio singing and playing guitar on the street corner and the smell of sausages grilling, Annie relaxed and enjoyed the time. Austin manned the booth with her, selling strawberries and talking up the coming weekend sale at The Barn Yard. He'd brought along some blueberries for people to sample, his own idea, and seemed to enjoy pitching the product.

As Annie worked, having fun at the same time, she wondered how many people would've recognized Mitch.

She also wondered what he was doing with his time alone at the farm.

Lulu purred. Satisfied, Mitch drove to Vaughn's house on Ryder Ranch land, pleased that he'd been able to fix his treasured vehicle and looking forward to time with his older brother. When Mitch left for Argentina, Vaughn had just finished building his house and moving in his wife and daughter after years of living and working in San Francisco. Now he was divorced and a single father.

The two-story, cedar-siding house fit the landscape perfectly, its wraparound porch welcoming. He'd landscaped with hardy evergreens and other low maintenance and drought-resistant plants, the same as their parents' house. A swing set, slide and climbing structure sat to one side, shaded by oaks that had preceded generations of Ryders.

Vaughn opened the screen door, stepping onto the porch as Mitch climbed the stairs.

"Everything looks great," Mitch said, greeting his brother with a strong hug.

"I'm glad I moved home. I think the only new structure since you left is the stables. Want to see it?"

"Sure." Their strides were even as they walked. His

brother hadn't planted anything edible, although there was plenty of land to do so. "Still not a gardener, I see."

"I don't understand anyone's need to dig in dirt," Vaughn said. "But since Mom does, I let her supply me with plenty of fresh vegetables. I do cook, you know. Cassidy and I don't starve, by any means."

The stable reflected Vaughn's life—orderly, organized and regimented. Walking into his bedroom when they were growing up was like walking into a military barracks. His stables were the same—and empty.

"They're in the corral out back."

They wandered that direction. Mitch recognized Vaughn's horse, Cody. "I take it the old lady horse is Cassidy's."

"Cass will tell you she's a pony, not a horse. She named her My Little." Vaughn grinned. "She was three. What can I say?"

"It's cute." They draped their arms over the corral fence and watched in silence for a minute.

"How was it?" Vaughn asked.

"Hard and healing."

"Mom about went crazy."

"I'm sorry about that, but not sorry I went. It was what I needed."

"And now? Are you ready to be back in the fold?"

"If it's folded differently, yes."

Vaughn eyed him. "What does that mean?"

"That I want more responsibility, more involvement in decisions, more credit."

Vaughn nodded. "I get that. He's a tough old bird, our dad."

"He learned from the best," Mitch said, laughing a little. "Granddad never budged an inch."

"Except with you."

Mitch shrugged acknowledgment. He'd learned that connections made in life often defied explanation. His with his grandfather was one of them. "I think you have Cassidy because of a similar connection. She's not your blood, but she's yours more than she was ever her mother's."

"True."

"Where does everything stand with you?"

"Divorce is final. Ginger's dropped out of sight. I'm trying to track down Cassidy's biological father so that I can end all potential legal difficulties. It hasn't been easy. Lots of dead ends."

They returned to the house, grabbed a couple of beers then sat on the porch. Vaughn passed him a folder, the pleased look on his face tipping Mitch off to the contents. Mitch whistled when he saw the bottom line. "How'd you manage this?"

"In ways that would've had you hyperventilating. You've never been willing to take risks with money. I prefer to, myself. There's your payoff."

Mitch already had a pretty good cushion in the bank since he rarely spent money on anything. "This'll go a long way toward my plans for my property. I can't thank you enough. You're right. I wouldn't have risked much."

"It's why I didn't let you know. Also why I told Mom and Dad not to tell you that Adam and Brody were paying rent. You would've had them plant it in your savings account. I couldn't let that happen."

"I take it you've done the same for yourself. You certainly can't support yourself on Ryder Ranch's legal needs."

"Can't and don't. I've taken on quite a few ranches in the area as clients. It's small business, but together it's enough. Doing a little family law, too, and some consulting online. It all adds up."

Mitch studied his brother. "Doesn't sound like it adds up to a social life."

Vaughn leaned back, crossing his ankles. "I don't know which of us got worse treatment by a woman, but I think we're equally jaded. At least I got Cassidy out of the deal. And I don't live like a monk." He grinned at Mitch. "Do you?"

"With Annie, you mean? There's nothing going on there. Hell, I've only known her for a week."

"So?"

"She's got a ten-year-old kid who's there all the time."

Vaughn laughed. "Meaning you would've been sleeping with the proud Ms. Barnard if the kid hadn't been around?"

"I didn't say that."

"You'd like to."

"Hell, yes. Unlike you, I *have* been living like a monk."

"And she is one fine-looking woman. If a little prickly."

"Not when you get to know her." Mitch debated how much to say to his brother, the person he trusted most—which decided it for him. "Yeah, I'd like to take her to bed, but I can't."

He went on to share the whole story about how he ended up at her place and what had happened since. It felt good to say it out loud, to feel nothing but interest from Vaughn, who lifted his bottle of beer in a kind of toast when Mitch stopped talking.

"Rock and hard place."

"Yeah," Mitch said.

"Damned if you do tell her. Damned if you don't."

"Definitely."

"Between the devil and the deep blue sea."

"Got any more clichés for me?"

"Fresh out. Ah, here comes dinner."

A little blue car with a sign attached to the top came up the driveway, kicking up dust.

"Aw, man. You remembered," Mitch said, his mouth watering. Roma's Pizza was the place he'd missed most. "Meat Lover's Delight?"

"Is there anything else on the menu?" Vaughn met the driver at his car, then returned with a jumbo-size box, which he set on a porch table. He went inside then returned with two more beers.

They lingered a long time, reminiscing, debating, analyzing and sharing. As Mitch drove to Annie's hours later, happiness settled in him, around him and through him. Her truck wasn't in sight, which surprised him. The market ended at seven. It was almost eight-thirty. But he'd no sooner parked than she rolled in.

He opened the driver's door, peering into the truck bed as he did. "How'd it go?"

"Great. We sold out. I had to hold a few things back so that I could trade for what we needed. Austin teased everyone with his sampling of blueberries. We even splurged and bought sausage sandwiches. And it looks like Brenna James is going to be a big buyer. I'm re-thinking my plans for the farm."

"In what way?"

"Let me work it out in my head first. Did you fix your truck?"

"Purring like a kitten."

"How exciting!" She hitched a thumb toward the back of her truck. "I got the roof repair materials."

Mitch wondered why she wasn't sharing her plans.

She didn't trust him? She'd used him as a sounding board before. Had something happened at the farmer's market to change that?

Austin came around the truck and hugged Mitch, saying everything without saying anything. Together they unloaded and put items away, including the things Annie had traded for—salad cucumbers, grape tomatoes, peaches and green beans. Then later, when Austin had gone to bed, Annie gave Mitch an envelope. "Your pay for the week."

He didn't want it. He was grateful for the place to stay while he worked out his issues and had no need of her money, whereas she had every need. Yet he couldn't hurt her pride by not accepting it. He would leave it behind when he left, but for now, he would accept it.

"Thanks," he said, stuffing the envelope in his pocket.

Her eyes shimmered. She'd had a successful and satisfying time at the market, was almost floating on air about it. "It's only going to get better, Mitch. I can feel it. I even told Ginny that. And I thanked her for recommending you."

She had to be talking about Ginny Otta, a local orchard grower who was active in the community, even leading the way to bring an important food summit to their area. She was a mover and a shaker, and their families had known each other forever.

Before he could say anything, Annie added, "Ginny told me you'd stopped by my farm the day before but had left, thinking there was too much work. That surprised me, because you've never shied away from hard work."

What she said explained a lot. And apparently neither Ginny nor Annie had mentioned him by name or the conversation would've been entirely different.

"I really was only delaying going home," Mitch said,

hoping that would satisfy her. "It was a tough decision, but I made the right choice."

"I agree." She grinned. "So, how did you spend your time off?"

"With my older brother. He loaned me some fishing gear, by the way. We had pizza at his house."

"How nice. What does he do?"

Mitch hesitated. She'd met his brother, the attorney. Would she make the connection, figure out why she thought she'd met him before? Mitch tried to keep his words as truthful as possible, although he acknowledged he was lying by omission, too. "He's a lawyer. He'd lived and worked in San Francisco until a few years ago when he decided he wanted to raise his daughter here where he grew up."

"So, he's married."

They'd been standing in the kitchen as they talked, Annie putting ingredients into her bread maker. "Not anymore."

She kept her back to him. "I hope he gets to see his daughter."

"He has full custody of her. Her mother is AWOL."

She shut the lid on the bread maker and pushed a couple of buttons, setting it to cycle through in time for breakfast. "I'm not sure what's worse—a parent who calls often enough to keep a tether but never follows through, or a parent who just disappears. Both are hard."

"Yeah."

She looked around, then faced him. "I'll shower now. Suddenly I'm exhausted."

She rested a hand on his arm as she passed by him. Sorry that her good mood had been shattered, he stopped her and pulled her close. Or at least that was all he'd intended—a comforting hug. But when her body came flush with his, need slammed into him. She burrowed in, tucking her face against his neck. Apparently a hug was enough for her.

But then she edged closer and pressed her lips to his chest above the top button of his shirt. He dropped his head back as she made a warm, wet trail with her tongue. Mitch slid his hands over her rear, cupping her, lifting her. He brought his mouth down on hers, her tongue seeking his instantly, sounds of pleasure mingling with their breaths. Again and again they changed angles, seeking impossibly closer contact. Her mouth was on fire. Her hands roamed his body, exploring, arousing, teasing.

"You're gritting your teeth," she whispered, looking pleased.

"I'm trying not to embarrass myself, but it feels too good to make you stop." He couldn't let her continue any longer, so he turned the attention on her instead, leaning against the wall and drawing her between his legs. Then he opened a few snaps of her blouse and slid a hand inside her bra. "You have an amazing body," he said. "Perfect in every way."

Annie struggled to breathe as he reached around her and unhooked her bra. He thumbed her nipples. Then finally he sucked one into his mouth, his tongue and teeth getting into the action. She curved her arms over his head, keeping herself from falling, preventing him from stopping. "That feels so good," she murmured, dragging out the words, feeling the ache between her legs become unbearable.

Then he touched her there, a mere touch, and her knees gave way. He caught her, held her and used his whole hand on her, his thumb pressing and circling where the ache centered. He kissed her as she climaxed, stifling the sounds she made, adding to the incredible sensations. His generosity brought pure pleasure and unmatched satisfaction, triggering an avalanche inside her. She'd been unsatisfied for years, then celibate. She couldn't get enough of him now.

Eventually awareness returned. "I can't believe we did that with Austin in the house," she said, fastening her blouse, her breasts feeling tender and swollen.

"Need can outweigh common sense." He straightened his own clothes.

"It never has before. Not for me." She realized what she'd just revealed to him—that no one else had satisfied her like that before—and wondered what he thought about that.

He cupped her face, kissed her gently. "Go shower. I'm going to cool off outside."

"Good night," she said as he walked away. *Sweet dreams.*

She hoped for the same for herself.

Chapter Twelve

Marissa and her children showed up for the first U-pick at The Barn Yard. Annie was disappointed her husband hadn't come along. She would've liked to have met him, compared him, actually. She was more than a little curious about the man Marissa had chosen after Mitch and why that marriage was so successful.

Austin was having the time of his life. Annie enjoyed watching him work the crowd, showing them how to choose and pick berries. He grew more confident by the moment, his pride in his work evident. They weren't overrun with customers by any means, but it was a steady crowd from eight to noon, enough to empty the vines of the ripe fruit. Annie mostly weighed the picked berries, and made change and small talk. She recognized more townspeople now, some of whom had become regular customers at the farmer's market. Many brought their children, giving them the experience of picking their own berries.

Mitch had taken off at seven o'clock, figuring—rightly—that people would start showing up early, including Brenna James, who picked a lot of blueberries, toured the facilities and listened to Annie's plans for expansion.

A pickup with the Morgan Ranch logo on the door pulled into the driveway close to eleven. Win Morgan hopped out and moseyed over to where Annie stood behind a small table.

He touched the brim of his hat. "Mornin', Ms. Barnard."

"Mr. Morgan. Did you come to pick berries?"

"Yep. I was driving by and saw your sign. What kind are you selling?"

"Blueberries and strawberries. Next week we'll have blackberries, too, if you like those." She passed him a basket, calling his bluff. She was almost positive he hadn't dropped by to pick berries. "My son can show you how to choose the ones that are ripe."

"I'm not a virgin at this," he said with that incredible smile of his. He was too handsome, she decided. Before he moved on, he lowered his voice and said, "Is this how you're gonna keep your farm?"

"It all adds up."

He stared at her for a few long seconds. When she didn't look away, he finally wandered off, a small smile on his lips. Under other circumstances she might have liked him, but he was a Morgan so he was the enemy, just like the Ryders. Land-grabbing, money-grubbing louts, all of them.

Win stopped to talk to Marissa for a minute. They were about ten years apart in age, Annie figured, so they probably hadn't been friends growing up, but since Marissa had been married to a Ryder, they most likely knew each other.

Marissa brought two baskets to the table. "Your conversation with Win Morgan looked intense. What does he want?"

"Berries, he said." She dumped the blueberries into a plastic bag then set it on the scale.

"Maybe he's interested in cougars."

Annie laughed. "Now hold on. I know I'm looking worn-out these days, but I can't be more than a few years older than him."

Marissa cocked her head. "It wouldn't hurt you to put on a little makeup, you know. Leave your hair down sometimes, curl it a little, at least when you're at the farmer's market. Or maybe you aren't interested in dating."

"I don't have time or interest, frankly." Which was a lie. She was pretty much obsessed with one man, who, although they hadn't repeated the intimacy of earlier in the week, only had to look at her to make her heat up, inside and out. They both occasionally touched each other's arm or shoulder as they passed by. Sometimes he would cup her rear for a second, if Austin wasn't around. She didn't need more than that to spend the rest of the day edgy and restless.

But since Monday, they hadn't kissed or embraced. She was going crazy with need.

"Pardon my directness, but wouldn't your life be a lot easier with a man to help?" Marissa asked.

"I told you I hired a handyman. My life has eased up some because of that."

"For chores, but how about for the other things we

need in life?" She wiggled her brows a few times, making Annie laugh.

"I'm making do."

"Well, if you'd fix yourself up just a little, you could be making whoop-de-do."

Annie grinned at the made-up term. "I'll think about it. People might talk if I make that kind of a change midseason of the market. They might think I'm after their husbands or something, just when I'm getting to be friends with many of them."

Marissa rolled her eyes. "You're crazy. Nobody will think that." She took her two bags of berries and her change then hollered at her kids to head to the car. "You come to town an hour early next Monday. We'll give you a not-too-dramatic makeover."

Annie tamped down her practical side to say shakily, "Okay."

"Great! I'll see you then."

What had she done? She'd made arrangements for a makeover with Mitch's ex-wife, who'd done him wrong in some big way. She would have to make an excuse to cancel.

Win set his basket on the table. The contents included five strawberries and about twenty blueberries. His expression dared her to comment, so she refrained. The blueberries hardly weighed enough to register.

"A dollar sixty-five," she said.

He handed her two dollars. "Keep the change. Your boy helped me choose the sweetest, he said."

Annie tucked the bills into her cash apron. "Thanks."

"Everything's looking good here, Ms. Barnard. You've put in a lot of work."

"This is my future."

He leaned close. "I'm not the enemy. In fact, I'm rooting for you. I admire anyone who builds something out of nothing."

"Not exactly nothing, Mr. Morgan. There was plenty here to start with. I've just improved it."

"You're too modest." He touched his hat. "Good day, Annie."

The easy way he'd said her first name annoyed her for a few seconds, then she decided it was a sign of respect—or admiration. He hadn't just been flattering her when he'd given the compliment. "Tell your father I said hello, Win," she called to him.

He turned around, grinning as he walked backward. "Will do."

Maybe she'd convinced the Morgans to give up pressuring her. Now if she could just do the same with the Ryders, who even had a lawyer in the family.

Those Ryders sure must get themselves into a lot of jams.

Mitch waited until two o'clock before he headed back to the farm, feeling completely rested. He'd even napped while leaning against a tree, his line dangling in a deep pool. A nibble woke him. He reeled that trout in and two more before he set aside his tackle and went for a swim. He hadn't had this much free time since...ever.

On Monday Adam and Brody would come help him fix the barn roof, then all the jobs on his list would be done. There would be no good reason to stay, even Annie would be able to see that. He wouldn't leave without giving her his last name. After that, he wouldn't be welcome anymore, not even to help with big jobs now and then, no matter how stretched she was.

He'd dug himself into a very deep hole without any means of extricating himself.

He wanted to sleep with her, but in an honest way. And eight days from tomorrow, Austin would leave for San Diego for a week. A week. Mitch could tell her in the truck on the way back from the airport. She would be stuck listening to him, giving him time to convince her he'd stayed with her because he wanted to help her succeed. Would she believe him?

Then there was the matter of their sleeping together just before he returned to his own house, his own work. Would she think he'd gotten what he wanted then moved on?

Tangled webs.

Mitch couldn't see any vehicles in front of the farm or at the end of the driveway. He eased in and found only Annie's truck. Austin raced out of the house as Mitch grabbed the thermal container from the truck bed.

"You caught some!" Austin bounded to a stop, waiting for Mitch to open the container then looking inside it. "Three big ones. Wow! Can we go tomorrow, since we're not working on Sundays anymore?"

"Your mom makes those decisions. How'd the picking go?"

"Awesome. We sold everything that was ripe. We had to turn away people at the end. They said they'd come earlier next week. Cool, huh?"

"Very. Where's your mom?"

"In the kitchen, canning tomatoes."

"Thanks. Stay out here, okay? I need to talk to her in private."

Mitch carried the cooler into the house, noting they'd already put the netting over the bushes again, keeping the birds out of the berries. The scent of cooked tomatoes filled the air, even with the windows open. When he walked into the kitchen he found her washing dishes, and the counter lined with full jars.

"You've been busy," he said, eyeing the bow of her apron as he had before, resting temptingly at the base of her spine. He wished he had the right to press his body to hers, to wrap his arms around her, to kiss her neck—

She spun around, a smile on her face. "Hey. How'd you do?"

He opened the lid. "I never asked if you like trout."

"One of my favorites."

"Austin said you had a good day."

She laid a hand on his arm and rubbed it, then slid it up to his shoulder, holding eye contact the whole time. "I missed you."

"Annie—"

She put a finger to his lips. "Did you miss me?"

He hesitated a beat. "You've become a habit."

Annie laughed. He'd rarely been off her mind all day. Although she'd committed to not having a man in her life until Austin graduated from high school, she'd gone and fallen in love with Mitch, a secretive stranger. She was either fortunate or foolish. She didn't know which yet. "A good or bad habit?"

"Little of both, I suppose." He glanced out the window, then he kissed her softly, tenderly, briefly, making her want so much more.

"Will you stay until Austin comes back from San Diego?" she asked.

After a moment he nodded.

They wanted the same thing, which excited her and also made her relax. She wouldn't have to worry about him leaving yet.

"Which leads into something I'd like to talk about," he said, setting the cooler in the sink. "I think it'd be good if Austin learned how to drive your tractor. If you don't mind, I'd like to teach him."

"Do you really think he's ready?"

"Farm kids all over America drive tractors, help with haying, other big chores like that. How many uses does your tractor have? It pulls the plow, guides the tiller, shovels snow and pulls other vehicles, when necessary. He should know how to do these things. For now, you don't have to let him haul anything, just till some of that land behind your house for practice. There's no pressing business this afternoon, is there? You know it's better than watching TV or playing on the computer."

Butterflies swarmed in her stomach. She wasn't ready for her boy to take on adult tasks, but that was the city girl in her. If he'd been raised on this farm, he would've assumed other roles long ago. "Okay. But if I see he's taking any chances—"

"You can't watch." He cupped her shoulders. "Just Austin and me. Then he can show off for you. He'll do better if he's not worried about what you're thinking. Or trying to show off for you. One's as bad as the other. I won't take him off the property."

She knew Austin would listen better to Mitch than her, and wouldn't talk back to him like he might her. "Uncle! You convinced me. I'll surf the internet for trout recipes."

"Oh, no, you won't. I'm barbecuing them."

Annie sighed. "I'll get the tractor key." She'd no more than passed by him when she felt her apron strings come untied and his large, sensual hands cup her rear.

"I've been wanting to do that since I first got here," he said. "You sure do fill out a pair of Wranglers."

She'd stopped, was holding on to the doorjamb and looking out the window, letting him touch all he wanted, enjoying every second. "Is that why you walk behind me so much?"

"I spend plenty of time checking out your front side, too, boss. I'm an equal opportunity ogler." He hooked a finger in her jeans, pulling her against him. "You don't have a bad side, by the way."

They both spotted Austin through the window, tossing a Frisbee for Bo. Annie made a quick move toward the front door, pushing open the screen, sensing Mitch right behind her.

"Austin, come over here a sec," she called.

He tossed the Frisbee again, sending Bo in the other direction.

"Mitch is going to teach you to drive the tractor. You have to—"

Austin jumped straight up and around in a circle at the same time, hollering *woohoo*. "Thanks, Mom."

"You have to listen to him, and do exactly as he tells you. The first time you decide you know more than him, he stops the lesson. Got it?"

"Yes, ma'am."

She laughed, giving him a playful shove. "Ma'am, indeed."

Annie didn't do as Mitch asked. She peeked out windows, watching Austin maneuver some narrow rows. She knew there wasn't much to driving the tractor, but it was high off the ground and without seat belts. Plus Austin had never driven any kind of vehicle. When she first drove the tractor, it had taken all her nerve and years of experience driving a car to feel comfortable, especially without the seeming safety of an enclosed vehicle.

She needn't have worried. He didn't make a single misstep that she could see, except maybe to give it too much gas a couple of times. She supposed that all his video game playing had given him some experience in maneuvering objects in and around small spaces and at a much higher speed than that old tractor could manage. At least that old 1970 John Deere was one she could repair herself, since it didn't have an electronic part anywhere.

Just when she was about to turn away she saw the bird netting catch on the smokestack and yank. She gasped, ran to the porch and was just about to holler when the engine shut down.

Mitch waved at her behind Austin's back, indicating she should go back in the house, then they didn't come in for a long time. She kept herself busy making a salad and prepping potatoes in foil packets for dinner so that Mitch could grill the fish and the potatoes at the same time.

Annie hadn't expected Austin to be perfect, especially when some of the rows were hardly wider than the tractor. It was better he'd found that out now and knew how to fix it. She just hoped the damage to the netting was minimal.

When she saw them parking the tractor later she busied herself in the kitchen again, making a peach cobbler. There was a new look in her son's eyes, the enthusiasm that was usually there but mixed now with pride of accomplishment. He was standing taller. Mitch had been right. Austin was ready.

"How'd it go?" she asked, as if she hadn't seen anything.

"Pretty good."

Annie glanced at Mitch, who leaned against the doorjamb, his arms crossed, his expression bland—except around his eyes, which sparkled with something, either amusement or lust. She didn't know which.

"Only pretty good?" Annie finally asked.

"I only goofed up once. The netting kinda got caught on the smokestack as I drove by the end of the row, so it kinda got dragged off the bushes."

"Were you able to fix it?"

"Yeah."

"Okay, then. Congratulations." She hugged her son, who fell against her for a couple of seconds, as if he'd been expecting her to lecture him or something. "Tomorrow you can start tilling the back field."

He hesitated. "Tomorrow's Sunday."

"Oh, that's right. Well, Monday, then." She waited for him to react, trying hard not to laugh. It was a struggle for him—take the day to go fishing or drive the tractor.

"Isn't tilling a spring job?"

"I'm trying to give you practice on the tractor," she said, a little surprised that he was arguing the point. "Don't you want to?"

He glanced at Mitch. "We hooked up the tiller and tried it out. It's kinda hard, and it's soooo slow, Mom. Mitch says I'll get stronger as I grow up, then it'll be easier."

"And that will help you drive it in straight lines, too?" Amused by her son, Annie kept after him.

"You know, there's this GPS made just for tractors to help drive in straight lines—"

Annie finally laughed. "In your dreams. We'll use stakes and string or whatever low-tech-but-free assistance we can get." She ruffled his hair. "Nice try, though."

He grinned then raced out of the house. After a few seconds he was tossing the Frisbee for Bo again.

"I've said it before. He's quite a kid," Mitch said.

"He has your sense of responsibility but still a child's enthusiasm."

"I hope he doesn't lose that as the burdens become heavier. The older he gets, the more I'll expect of him."

"Hard work never hurt me. He'll do fine, and be better for it down the road. Small farm growers are aging out in this country. We'll need young blood to keep it going."

"I have to make The Barn Yard profitable for him to be interested."

"You keep insisting you will."

If I had a man like you by my side, I would be sure of it. No, not a man like you, but you in particular. "I'm optimistic by nature."

"I've noticed. And stubborn. That's quite a one-two punch." He pushed away from the door. "I'll go start the charcoal."

Annie watched him leave, wondering at his thoughtful mood, but decided not to try to make something of it. She turned back to the peach cobbler she'd started, relaxed and happy, humming, not thinking about the tune until it struck her.

She stopped singing for a moment, then smiled. Yes, it was nice to have a man around the house.

Chapter Thirteen

Annie didn't tell Mitch why she and Austin were leaving early for the farmer's market two days later. It would even be a surprise for Austin until they got into the truck. He could spend time with his friend Ben while Annie let herself be made over by Marissa.

It was the craziest thing she could remember doing. She'd picked up the phone several times to cancel then hung it up again. She knew Mitch was as attracted to her as she was, but she was thirty years old. It was time to let go of the makeup-free face and easy ponytail, at least when she wasn't working in the fields.

Austin provided directions to Marissa's house, which was in a hilly part of town. The houses in the neighborhood were about a hundred years old and large, with lots of rooms. Marissa's home had great curb appeal, both the structure and the front garden, with plenty of blossoming plants.

So Marissa's trip to the farm really hadn't been about buying a bouquet from Annie but about forming a friendship, because she had a wonderful cutting garden herself.

"You have a green thumb," Annie said as Marissa came down the porch steps, and Austin raced up them to where Ben was waiting.

"I don't. My husband does. I kill plants just looking at them." Her cheeks flushed a little. "I guess you figured out it was a total ruse coming to your place."

"I'm honored."

Marissa gave Annie a tour of the charming home, with its Victorian/shabby-chic design that suited her. A large family portrait in a gilded frame hung over the fireplace, providing Annie's first glimpse of Marissa's husband, who was as opposite from Mitch as a man could be.

"That's my sweet John," Marissa said, smiling fondly at the portrait. He looked a good ten years older than she, with a sturdy build and bald head. His smile was framed by dimples and his eyes sparkled. He looked… content, she decided. Happy.

"You have a beautiful family," Annie said.

"Thank you. I tried my hardest to push John away. He refused to go. Then he got me pregnant, so I couldn't go, either. I know, I know. Maybe I sort of didn't remind him about protection a few times. What can I say? After my divorce from Mitch, I thought I didn't deserve to be loved, but John would have none of that."

"He sounds wonderful."

"He put up with a lot in the beginning." She led the way to her bedroom, where the makeover would take place. "He was already a successful businessman when we met. He owned a company that produced a product made by only two companies in the world, and then he bought out the other one. Then he sold it. Now he could retire if he wanted. At forty-nine! It's crazy. But of course, he wouldn't know what to do with himself. He's figuring out what he wants to do next."

"How did you meet?"

"In Sacramento, where I'd moved after the divorce. He came into the beauty shop where I was working. His regular stylist had to leave unexpectedly, so I cut his hair. Yes, he had hair then, although not a lot. I was the one to convince him to shave off what was left. He could've done it himself from there on, but he came in every week, and every week he asked me out until he finally wore me down."

She told Annie to sit on a stool she'd brought to her bathroom. "May I cut your hair a little? I'll leave it long enough to pull into a ponytail, but give you a more modern look."

Annie hadn't had a professional cut in too many years to count. She occasionally trimmed her ends, but she knew it wasn't even. She'd had Austin help the last time, but he'd been too nervous to finish. "Okay," she said, blowing out a nervous breath.

"I won't butcher it. I promise."

Marissa dampened Annie's hair and started in. Annie didn't look in the mirror until her hair had been blow-dried and styled.

"Oh, I love it! I just love it." She shook her head, the shoulder-length ends moving, fluttering, then settling again, looking even blonder and shinier. Only then did she look at the floor and frowned. "Where'd my hair go? You had to take a ton off. There's only a little."

Marissa dangled a clump, then put a rubber band around it. "We'll donate this. There's enough. I figured if I told you I'd be taking off eight inches you'd object. But you needed it."

Next came the makeup. She didn't put anywhere near as much on Annie as she used on herself, and Annie was pleased with the results. "You're a magician."

"Everyone needs a life skill." Marissa smiled into the mirror, meeting Annie's gaze. "I need to ask you a question."

"Okay."

"You never ask me about my first marriage, even though I've given you plenty of openings. Why is that? Does it remind you of your own? Does it still hurt too much?"

The direct question threw Annie. So far, she'd avoided lying. "That's three questions," Annie answered with a halfhearted smile. The truth was, she didn't want to know. Not from her about him, or from him about her. She liked Marissa, and she'd fallen in love with Mitch. Both relationships seemed destined to fail.

She squeezed Marissa's hand. "Mine ended only a year ago," she said, hoping Marissa would think it was still too painful, as she'd guessed.

"Okay. Some other time."

Annie glanced at an ornate little clock on the vanity and hopped up. "I need to get going. Thank you so much."

"My pleasure. Would it help if I send the boys with you to help set up?"

"Austin and I have it down to a science, but thank you. I'll be in touch."

"Ooh, la la," Ginny Otta said when Annie climbed out of her truck. "Going to a ball, Cinderella?"

"I'm short a pair of glass slippers."

"Oh, so those were yours? A prince was here looking for you, but he just left."

Austin had climbed into the truck bed and was passing the booth pieces to her. "The fractured fairy tale of my life," Annie said with a sigh.

Ginny laughed and went back to constructing her own booth. Brenna James came early, as usual, but this time was carrying a covered container. "Tell me what you think."

She'd brought a green salad with blueberries, roasted slivered almonds, red onion and the shallot vinaigrette she'd spoken about the last time. Annie closed her eyes, savoring the flavors. "Perfect," she said. "Absolutely perfect."

"It was the special Saturday night. Everyone loved it. The fingerlings, too."

"How did you fix them?"

"A combination of roasting and steaming, then tossed with a lemon, herb and olive oil dressing, very light, served hot, and alongside a perfect rib eye."

"Beef? Really?"

"Organic doesn't mean vegan. Have you heard of Ryder Ranch? It's local."

Annie stopped the sarcastic response that came to her first. "I'm familiar with them."

"Do you know they're one of only three cattle ranches in the country certified as humane and organic? Their beef is perfection. I don't use anything but theirs. They have a closed herd. That matters to me." She picked through the lettuce, filling a bag. "I'd like to have a meeting with you sometime soon. I think we could help each other out."

It took Annie a few seconds to respond. She'd been

stuck on the idea of the Ryders being humane about anything. "Anytime, Brenna."

"Give me a week. I'm having company for a few days, plus I've got some thinking to do."

"You sure do know how to tease a girl."

Brenna smiled. "Speaking of *girl,* you're looking young and rested."

"I got my hair cut. A little makeup does wonders, too."

"Mmm, yes, maybe." She didn't look convinced. "It's something deeper than that. You look happy."

I'm in love! Annie wanted to shout it to the rooftops. Her world was brighter, at times she even felt weightless. She found herself smiling more, talking more, not just to the vendors but the customers. The hours flew by. She was having a great time.

She also couldn't wait to get home.

"Bring up that can of tar, wouldja, Adam?"

Mitch watched his brothers as they patched the barn roof then traipsed all over the rooftop seeking anything in need of sealing. He envied their ease on the roof, as sure-footed as goats on a mountain.

"I'm no roofer, Mitch," Brody said, "but I don't think this will hold more'n a couple more years. If that. It's gotta be fifty years old, and it's been repaired a lot."

"I'll tell her, thanks." He was barbecuing an entire meal on the grill—trout that he and Austin had caught yesterday, potatoes, corn on the cob and a loaf of garlic bread, everything wrapped in foil. There was ice cream in the freezer, if any of them had room for it.

By the time dinner was done, so were his brothers. They washed up, loaded their plates and sat on the front porch as they demolished the food. They'd already put in a long day of work at the ranch before they'd come.

"You planning on comin' home anytime soon?" Brody asked. "Dad's expecting you for the hayin' for sure, and Adam and I need to know if we should make other living arrangements."

"What are your options?"

"Bunkhouse or Mom and Dad's."

"Neither one is good for privacy," Mitch said, studying his corn as he considered their situation. "You don't have girlfriends you can move in with?"

"I just broke up with Betsy. Adam's never had a relationship longer'n two months."

Adam shrugged. "So many girls. So little time."

"Let's not make a decision now," Mitch said. "When I move home, we'll talk about it."

"So, *will* you be there for the hayin'?"

"Yeah." He owed his father that much. Many hands were needed. Although some of their properties were miles away, he would make sure he stayed local so that he could come back to the farm each night.

"As long as it's not next week," Mitch said. Next week he hoped to be makin' hay with Annie most of the time.

"Week after, looks like."

"All right."

From his spot curled up next to Mitch, Bo came to attention. A pickup approached, but from a distance it looked like most trucks in these parts.

"It's Vaughn," Adam said.

"Am I too late for dinner?" Vaughn asked as he climbed out of the truck.

"You're too late to help, so you're too late for dinner," Brody said.

Vaughn held up two six-packs of beer. "Ice-cold."

"Well, then, I guess we can make an exception."

There was enough food left, and the four brothers, who hadn't been together for three years, kicked back, told stories and enjoyed their lifelong connection.

Contentment, even happiness, washed over Mitch. It was good to be home. He'd missed his brothers, missed his life on the ranch, missed the comfort of knowing they had each others' backs, anytime, anywhere.

"Anyone hear from little sister Jenny?" Mitch asked.

"I talk to her frequently," Vaughn said. "She'll be home for winter break, then she'll go back for her last semester."

"Who would've thought it?" Mitch wondered aloud. "She'll have a degree in farm management. I always figured her for something in the arts, like Mom. She's got talent there."

"Hard to make a living as an artist," Vaughn said. "She's being practical."

Around seven-thirty, Mitch chased his brothers off and cleaned up the dishes. He'd started waxing his truck earlier and went back to working on it. Soon Annie and Austin drove in.

Bo raced to meet them, making happy sounds, his tail wagging. Mitch felt the same. He walked to Annie's side of the truck. She didn't open the door until he reached it, then he took a step back.

"You cut your hair."

She tossed her head a little. "What do you think?"

He was no fool. Even if he'd hated it, he wouldn't have said so. As it was, he liked it. A lot. "It looks great. Why'd you decide to do that?"

"Mrs. Mazur convinced her," Austin said, bounding around the truck to hug Mitch hello. "She did a make-over on Mom."

Mitch noticed Annie had on some makeup, too. Or at least eye shadow and lipstick.

Austin ran across the yard, letting Bo chase him. Annie seemed to be waiting for Mitch to say something.

"I didn't realize you'd become such close friends, after all," he said.

Annie laid a hand on his arm. "We're not, although I know she'd like to be. You don't need to worry. I don't talk to her about you. Honestly, I don't want to know. That's between you and her. Anyway, from the few things she's said, I gather she's the villain."

That word struck Mitch hard. Was she a villain? She'd been young, they both were. "One person can't cause all the problems in a marriage. It takes two."

"You're right about that. So," she said in a tone that indicated she was changing the subject, "I sold out again. And Brenna James wants to have a meeting with me soon about a business opportunity. She expects me to wait to hear exactly what that opportunity is! How am I going to pass the time while I'm sitting on pins and needles?"

He leaned close. "I can help you think of other things next week."

"I never thought the day would come when I would be happy to have my son gone for a week." She added in a whisper, "I think you'd better pick up another box of condoms."

"You dream big."

She smiled, sure and sexy. "I got up close and personal once. My dreams are realistic."

"It's gonna be a long six days, Annie."

"But think of the reward at the end of it."

"I think about little else." He walked around to the

back of the truck, needing to stop the tense discussion, and lowered her tailgate. "Your barn roof is fixed."

She spun around, taking a look. "Show me."

He walked with her into the barn. The sun was still up high enough that if there'd been holes or gaps, light would've shone through. She pressed her hands to her cheeks as she stared.

"Thank you so much, Mitch. How did you manage it?"

"I called in the cavalry. In this case, a couple of my brothers. I paid them with a barbecue. They're easy." He grinned. "Just so you know, I'm going to help them with the haying. That'll be the week Austin comes back. I'll be here at night, though."

"You've made contact with your family, which is what you've been resisting. Seems to me you're ready to go home."

"If you're looking at just the facts, that would seem to be true. But this isn't a black-and-white situation."

Mitch didn't want to get into this discussion now. He wanted his week with her, and he knew she wanted the same. Why create a possible disruption to something they both wanted so much? It would be better to leave things unsaid at this point.

"A day at a time, Annie," Mitch said.

After a moment she smiled. "That's what I always say, too."

"Okay. Let's get you unloaded. I promised Austin we'd have a video tournament using the game of his choice tonight. Gotta go warm up my thumb."

"And your reaction speed."

"Hey! I'm not doddering yet."

"Tell me that in about an hour." She sashayed to the

truck, looking over her shoulder once and smiling as if she knew everything there was to know in the world.

All he knew for sure was that he never got tired of looking at her.

Chapter Fourteen

Annie was glad Mitch volunteered to stay in the truck at the Medford Airport. It was hard enough letting Austin fly off, but she had to face Rick for the first time since their divorce was final. She had permission to go to the gates because Austin was a minor, so Austin waited impatiently at the window where Rick's flight was supposed to arrive. Annie sat nearby.

Most people thought Austin looked like her, but she'd always seen Rick in him. He moved like his father, especially when he walked. His mouth was all Rick. His ears stuck out the same.

She remembered back to when they'd met. She'd just graduated from high school. Her parents had given her the gift of staying in one place for the last two years she was in high school before taking off, leaving her to fend for herself. She'd had a thousand dollars, a waitressing job at a local diner and found an apartment to rent with three other girls. It'd been chaos, not only with her roommates, but their boyfriends, everyone coming and going at all times of the night.

She'd met Rick when he came into the diner, and after a month of dating, he swept off her to Reno and married her. They settled down in Fresno, where they'd both been living. The peacefulness of sharing an apartment with only one person was wonderful, but it wasn't too long before he found another job and they moved to Bakersfield. Then Sacramento, then Oakland, then finally back to Reno, where they'd been for three years before moving to The Barn Yard. Austin adapted well with each move. She'd stopped being able to.

Rick had been in San Diego for close to two years, so she figured he would be ready to move on soon.

"It's here! The plane's here!" Austin's happy voice took Annie out of her memories.

She joined him at the gate, waited for Rick to emerge. She'd just about decided he'd missed the flight when she spotted him.

"Dad!" Austin raced to the tall, thin man and threw himself at him, hugging him hard.

Rick made eye contact with Annie and smiled. He looked more civilized than she could remember. He wasn't wearing a suit, but he was dressed better than he used to, and his hair was styled, but with lots of gray in it. He looked...successful.

He gave Annie a quick, one-armed hug. "You're looking good, doll. You cut your hair."

"I could say the same of you. How was the flight?"

"Long. Dull. It'll be different on the way home." He rubbed Austin's head. "You've grown a few inches."

Annie was glad to see their easy rapport. She was afraid the time that had elapsed, as well as Rick's resentment of having to fly to get Austin, would make things strained, but Rick seemed fine, and Austin was obviously over-the-moon ecstatic.

"Our flight's not for an hour. Want to get some coffee?" Rick asked.

"Mitch is waiting," Austin said, then seemed to realize maybe he shouldn't have.

"Mitch?" Rick repeated.

"A handyman who helps out at the farm," Annie said calmly. "We need some building materials, so he came with us. We'll shop after you leave. He knew what time the flight was. I'm sure he expects me to stay until it's taken off. Which is a long way of saying yes, coffee would be fine."

They spent a surprisingly pleasant half hour together before they gathered at the gate for takeoff. Rick didn't reveal anything about his life. Not what kind of work he was doing, or whether he was dating. Nothing. Annie realized she didn't care. As long as he kept in touch with Austin and made him feel loved, it didn't matter how Rick lived his life.

She teared up when Austin hugged her goodbye, then they locked pinky fingers and whispered their mantra. "Have a great time, honey. Call when you get there, please."

"I will. Bye." He was antsy, wanted to get going on his adventure.

She said goodbye to Rick, then moved to the window and stood there until the plane pulled away from the gate and taxied off. It wasn't long before the plane took to the air. Only then did she make her way to the parking lot.

Mitch was sitting on the tailgate in the shade. He hopped down, and she walked straight into his arms. He didn't say a word, no platitudes, no trying to coax her into smiling. He just held her until she finally stepped back and swiped at her tears.

He took her face in his hands and brushed her cheeks with his thumbs, then he kissed her, the gentlest kiss anyone had ever given her. It made her want to cry all over again, but she screwed up her courage and said she was ready to go.

They did have errands—chicken feed and dog food to pick up, groceries to buy. She noticed he looked around all the time, as if he might see someone he knew, but no one said hello.

"Ready to go home?" he asked.

Neither of them had said much, which settled a different layer of tension over them, adding to the sexual tension that had built for weeks.

"I am *so* ready."

He reached across the seat to grab her hand. "How long until Austin calls?"

"Their flight stops in San Francisco first. They won't get to San Diego for hours. I'm guessing we'll have five hours from when they took off until he's settled at Rick's." They'd spent some time shopping, and the drive took a little more than hour. They could be leisurely, take their time, enjoy every second.

It didn't matter that they had a whole week of pleasure ahead of them. This would be their first time, and it needed to be memorable.

In the end, however, she couldn't wait for—and didn't need—any foreplay. She was ready to just do it then take it slower the second time. As they reached her driveway, she said those very words out loud.

Mitch had different ideas. He'd been thinking about this for a long time, and knew exactly how he wanted to proceed. She wasn't the boss in this situation.

He smiled at her and shook his head. "It matters to me that this is done right," he said. "Doesn't it matter to you?"

"In my head, yes. The rest of me is arguing like crazy."

He laughed, low and soft, as he pulled into the yard, grateful no one was there, waiting. People seemed to be surprising her with visits these days. He hoped this wouldn't be one of those days. He took her by the hand and walked her into the house, letting Bo out and shutting the door behind him. He'd be their alarm should a visitor arrive.

The day was warm, but not exceptionally so for August. They went directly into her bedroom. He shut the door and opened the window. A breeze fluttered the curtains. Together, they pulled the top sheet off the bed, leaving an inviting expanse. Bo whimpered outside the window.

"He's wondering where his boy went," Annie said as Mitch cupped her head. He lowered his mouth to hers and was immediately swept away. She tasted good. He'd noticed earlier that she wore perfume, only the second time he could remember her doing that, and as he nudged her ear with his nose, the scent rose to meet him. Her skin was hot and damp. He craved her.

His brain was imprinted with the time in her kitchen when he'd seen her breasts, touched them, tasted them. This time there would be no clothing between them, nothing to hide behind, no need to stay partially dressed in case someone came in. He could feel her struggle to breathe as he unbuttoned her blouse and peeled it off her. Reaching behind her, he unhooked her bra. She shrugged it down her arms, letting it fall to the floor.

Her nipples were a dusky rose against her pale skin.

He cupped her breasts, felt their solid weight in his hands. "Beautiful," he said.

She closed her eyes, her body softening. Obviously, she needed words, not just actions. Hadn't she been told how beautiful she was? How sexy? How perfect?

She laid her hands over his. "They used to be perkier. Having a baby, nursing—"

"Shh." He bent low, moved her hands to her sides and held them there, then he pulled a nipple into his mouth, savoring her. "You are perfection."

She made a long, low sound, more of a moan than a sigh, and he continued with what he was doing until she grabbed at his shirt, tugging it free of his jeans. He unsnapped it in one motion, yanked it off and came skin to skin with her.

"You have a perfect chest," she said, dragging her tongue over it, circling his nipples, biting them as she unbuckled his belt and unzipped his jeans.

They managed to get their boots off without laughing too much, then their jeans were commingling on the floor, their underwear landing on top.

"You need to get the condoms," she said suddenly.

"I put them under your pillow this morning."

"Well, darn. I wanted to see you walk away. And then walk back. You are a sight to see."

He accommodated her, saw the admiration in her eyes as he walked back, and was more turned on than he could ever remember being.

Still, he wanted to take his time.

"How can you hold back?" she asked as they lay side by side, facing each other on the bed.

He didn't tell her the truth—that he was thinking about what if this was the only time they got? What if someone who knew him interrupted them today and the dangerous game he'd been playing and she'd been going along with was over? He wanted the best memory possible—for her and himself.

"When something's important, you find a way to do the right thing, the right way. Just don't touch me," he added with a smile, lifting her hair from her face with his fingers. "Then all bets would be off. And so would I."

"Then we would seem to be at an impasse, neither of us able to touch."

"Who said I wasn't going to touch?" To prove his point, he dragged her leg over his then moved his hand between her legs. She arched back, dug her fingers into his shoulders and groaned. He took his hand away, watched her grit her teeth, wallowed in the pleasure he knew he was giving her.

"I can't take any more," she said, barely getting the words out. "I really can't."

She moved her hand blindly under a pillow then tossed the strip of condoms at him. "Put one of these on right now or I'll do it."

"Yes, boss."

She laughed, a shaky, lust-filled sound. Then she propped herself on her elbows and watched him make quick work of the protection. "You're way too efficient at that."

"If you only knew how many times as a teenager I practiced that move to get good at it."

"That's sweet."

He flattened her on her back, poised himself above her, felt her legs wrap around him and pull him down to her, guiding him to her at the same time. They climaxed together starting the moment he was inside her, kissing frantically, gripping each other hard. He arched and pushed as it went on and on, for both of them.

Oh, yeah, if this was the only time...this was perfect.

Finally he collapsed on her. After a few seconds, he rolled with her so that she could be on top. She snuggled against him, her legs nestled between his, her arms wrapped around him. He dragged his hands down to grip her rear, holding on.

"That was good," he said, in the biggest understatement of his life. "Really good."

"I have to agree with you."

"Give me a little time and we'll do it again." He almost growled the words, already mentally wanting her again, if not physically capable.

"I thought you'd never ask."

He laughed, stroking her body everywhere he could reach, enjoying every inch of her. Radiant heat flowed from him, not from below his waist, but from the middle of his chest, thawing the ice that had been wrapped around his heart for so long.

"I'm starving," she said, folding her arms on his chest and resting her chin on them, looking at him. "For food. Are you?"

Her hair was mussed. Mascara darkened the skin under her eyes here and there. She looked beautiful.

"I could eat," he said.

"We should probably put on some clothes, in case someone drops in."

"If we must."

She smiled first, then she pulled herself up his body far enough to kiss him. He wrapped her tight and rolled over, still kissing. She made the best cushion....

"Wanna play hooky and go fishing?" he asked.

"I'd like to be home when Austin calls. How about if we go tomorrow?"

"Okay. We could skinny-dip."

She laughed and shook her head as she climbed out of bed and grabbed her clothes, tossing him his.

"Is that a no?" he asked. "I've never seen a soul there."

"There's a swing rope. People go there." She stood still as he stopped dressing himself to hook her bra. Again she wished she had some pretty lingerie, but was resigned to the fact she couldn't afford to splurge on any.

"You could get into the water then take off your suit."

She shook her head again, but gave him points for not giving up easily. They finished dressing. She headed to her bedroom door, then found herself flattened against the wall next to it and being thoroughly and delightfully kissed.

"What do you wear to bed?" he asked against her mouth.

"Why do you want to know?"

"Because I've been wondering about it since the first morning when you came into the kitchen wearing your robe. Every so often I could see a bare leg. I was curious."

"Short summer pajamas. How about you?"

"Here? Underwear. In my own place alone? Nothing."

"I've never slept in the nude."

He pulled back, surprised. "Never?"

She toyed with his shirt collar. "What would happen if I go naked tonight?"

"At the least you'll find me wrapped around you, skin to skin. I don't care how warm it is."

"And at the most?"

"I expect one of us will be waking the other at some

point. But that would happen even if you wore long johns that buttoned everywhere. You're not gonna be safe from me until Austin gets back."

"Is that a promise?"

"Promise, guarantee, oath. Or possibly a threat, depending on how you look at it. Choose one."

She looped her arms around his neck. "*Threat* sounds dangerous."

"A threat's just a promise with more passion."

"Then I'll take the threat, please."

He laughed at her politeness. "Feel free to issue your own threats in return."

She went silent for several seconds. He waited her out, not trying guess what was on her mind.

"You haven't asked any questions about my marriage," she said finally.

"I figured you'd tell me what you wanted me to know."

"I don't have much to say about it, except this one thing, because it relates to you." She stepped back, reaching for his hands, keeping contact. "My sexual relationship with Rick was nothing like you and I just had, and that was our first time. It's hard to imagine it'll get even better with practice, but I guess it will. I've never really had the freedom to, you know, explore or experiment."

"Well, I want you to feel free to put me under your microscope. Prove any hypothesis you've been pondering. Consider your bedroom your laboratory."

She laughed and kissed him, then hauled him out of the room. Bo scratched at the front door, hearing them. He came flying inside, raced down the hall to Austin's room, then came back out slowly, his claws tapping the floor.

"He'll be home before you know it," Mitch said, scratching the dog's ears. "I had a dog as a kid, too, who missed me like crazy when I left for college and was always thrilled when I came home."

"I didn't know you went to college," Annie said as she washed her hands at the kitchen sink.

"All six of us have. Our parents required it."

She pulled out leftover meat loaf, the bread left from breakfast and a few tomatoes for hot meat loaf sandwiches. "What'd you major in?"

"I double majored in range ecology and animal science."

She gave him a steady look. "Why aren't you working in your field?"

"I am. Maybe not this second, but most of my career has involved what I learned in college—plus many more years of experience. How about you?" he asked, wanting to distract her from asking more personal questions.

"No college, but I've read a hundred books on farming, and thousands of articles, and talked to experts, educating myself. I've been thinking I should have a website built, not to draw the public but for people like Brenna, organic restaurant owners and maybe small specialty grocers. As soon as I get certified I can go after that business, but I figure I should be ready to go with the site ahead of time. What do you think?"

"I think you're smart and savvy." He grabbed plates from the cupboard and glasses to pour iced tea.

"I'll ask at the farmer's market tomorrow, see if anyone can recommend a designer. Or maybe I'll tackle it on my own. It doesn't have to be fancy."

"It has to look professional in order for others to see you as a professional. That's important."

While she warmed the meat loaf, he sliced tomatoes. "Mustard? Ketchup?" he asked, opening the refrigerator.

"Both, please."

They took their plates to the dining room. "It's weird with Austin gone," Annie said. "He always fills up the space with conversation."

"Worried we won't have anything to talk about?" Mitch asked.

"I think we would have a lot more if there weren't any barriers between us."

Ah. He'd wondered how long it would take. Maybe he'd been right. Maybe they'd made love for the first and last time. He set his sandwich on the plate. "You told me you didn't want to know my name."

"Yet. But that was also before I slept with you. Why do I have the feeling everything will be different when I find out?"

He didn't say anything, because the only thing he could honestly say was, "Yes, it'll be different." He knew she didn't want to hear that.

She took a bite of her sandwich, studying him thoughtfully as she chewed. He picked his up again. Neither of them said anything until they were finished.

"I've made a decision," she said finally.

Chapter Fifteen

Annie saw Mitch's fists clench where they rested on the table. He was a good, decent person. She didn't believe whatever revelations he had were all that horrible. They'd just gotten caught up in the deception and now were paying for it. It would turn out okay. She knew it would.

"You know how sometimes something happens that there's just no going back from? You can't turn back the clock? You have to live with your choice?"

"Yes," he said without hesitation.

"That's what's happened here. The opportunity has passed. We'll stick with the plan," she said. "For now."

She could see he didn't think they were doing the right thing, which made her even more afraid of what the truth was. But this time she would be selfish. She hadn't been selfish in a very long time.

"Now that the decision is made, let's leave it behind and enjoy the week," she said. "Deal?"

"Nothing would please me more, boss," he said with a quick grin, setting a new tone. He pushed his chair back, grabbed her hand and tugged her onto his lap, straddling him. "Do you ride?" he asked, cupping her rear, steadying her.

"Maybe if we were naked."

He tipped his head back and laughed. "I meant horses, but I do like the way you think."

"Oh." It was hard to think when he was unbuttoning her blouse. "Once. Years ago. Not my finest hour. That horse knew I was afraid of him before I even climbed into the saddle."

He let her blouse hang open but didn't touch her. His breath fell on her bare skin, warm and arousing.

"I know it's too late today," he said. "Especially since you need to be here for Austin's call, and tomorrow is taken up with the farmer's market, so how about Tuesday after chores I borrow a couple of horses and take you for a ride. We can pack a picnic lunch. I'll show you a different place on the river, accessible only by horseback. If you feel like skinny-dipping, you can. If not, you can watch me."

"I do love watching you naked," she said. She didn't think she'd ever get tired of that.

"You took the words out of my mouth." He ran his fingertips along her bra, dipping into her cleavage.

She wriggled a little, trying to get more comfortable. "You were wrong. You didn't need much time at all."

"You put a spell on me." He dipped his tongue between her breasts. "Are you seducing me back into your bed?"

"You're the one who pulled me onto your lap and un-buttoned my blouse."

"Oh, yeah." He grinned. "I forgot. But just so you know, you seduce me just looking at me."

"Ditto." She pressed a kiss to his mouth, sought his tongue with hers, was transported into another world. He managed to get her blouse and bra off her, then his hands and fingers were busy exploring. He added the warm wetness of his mouth, and she arched back, thoroughly enjoying his attentions.

"Wanna go to your room?" he asked.

She pressed her forehead to his and nodded. "Sometime when it's dark, and the curtains are drawn, and there's little chance of anyone dropping in, I want to do this again—without clothes."

"It's a date."

He stood, swinging her into his arms, and walked toward the bedroom. The phone rang.

"It's too early for Austin," she said.

He lowered her enough to grab the phone but didn't let go of her. It was all she could do not to giggle as she said hello.

"Hey, Annie, it's Ginny. Listen, I know I promised I'd help you set up and take down tomorrow since your son's gone, but my husband is in the hospital having an emergency appendectomy. Just wanted to give you a heads-up, so you can get someone else to help."

Mitch sat down in a nearby chair, still holding her, but otherwise not touching or teasing her, content to wait her out, not willing to let her go now that he had her. Fantasies did come true. He'd been creating scenarios in his head for weeks about her. They'd barely scratched the surface of those vivid scenes, but he figured most of them would be satisfied during the days ahead. She was more than willing.

A part of him was pleased he was satisfying her in ways she'd never been before, and a part of him was sorry for her about that. She'd been denied for too long. He intended to change that.

After she said goodbye, he took the phone from her and hung it up. "Bad news?"

"Just a little extra work tomorrow at the market. No big deal. Now, where were we?"

But the phone rang before he could move. As he listened to her side of the conversation, he realized they needed to put a second round of lovemaking on hold for now. He gathered up her bra and blouse, then helped dress her as she talked.

"Sounds like you need to change plans," he said when she hung up.

"Four of us are going to harvest Ginny's crops for market. Then tomorrow we'll go early and set up her booth, too."

"I'm sorry I can't help."

"It's okay. I won't leave until Austin calls, which should be fairly soon."

"I'm going to work on reorganizing the barn. I've been planning how it could be changed around a bit."

"Really? Thanks."

"You know, you never answered me about going riding on Tuesday."

"You noticed."

He took her hands. "You're scared. I see that. I know where I can get a very gentle mare, and I'll be right next to you." He crouched a little to get her to look at him. "This should be a week of all kinds of adventures, Annie."

"Okay, okay. But can we make it later in the week? And don't blame me if I'm too sore to fool around afterward."

"I can work around that. Bet you don't complain once." He left the house, leaving her to ponder his words, satisfied with how everything was going.

He was happy, too, something he was afraid to trust.

He'd been working in the barn for about a half hour when Annie joined him, keys in hand.

"Austin just called, so I'm going now."

"Is he okay?"

"He sounded subdued, actually."

"Jet lag?"

"I don't know. I had a feeling Rick was standing right there."

"He'll be fine. He's probably homesick."

She nodded, then kissed him. "See you in a while."

"I'm pretty sure you're gonna need a shower when you get back. And I know for sure that I will."

She just grinned and sashayed away. Oh, yeah, her soaped-up body would make for a great playground.

Mitch measured and cut planks to build some rough shelves, along with cement blocks he found. Storage space was almost nonexistent, but she needed lots. He measured and cut, running the circular saw time and again.

Which is why he didn't hear anyone drive in, or even Bo barking. But suddenly Marissa was standing just inside the barn door staring at him. She looked a little older, but also the same.

And he felt nothing. No anger, no hurt, no attraction.

"What are you doing here?" she asked. "Wait. Are you Annie's handyman?"

"For the moment." He walked over to her.

"She never said anything. I told her we'd been married...."

"Did you ever say my last name?"

She frowned. "I don't know. Why?"

"She doesn't know it. I saw you when your son was video-chatting with Austin, and I told Annie we'd been married. Look, I know you're becoming friends. I haven't said anything about you."

"I think you need to start at the beginning. Why doesn't she know who you are?"

They sat on a couple of hay bales, and he laid it out for her, trusting her, figuring she didn't want to hurt Annie any more than he did.

"This is a risky game you're playing, Mitch. I can tell you have feelings for her. You should tell her. The sooner, the better."

"One more week."

"Why? Oh. Austin's gone. I get it." She stood. "I won't say anything to her or anyone else, so you can rest easy about that."

"Why'd you come?"

"I figured she'd be having a hard time her first night alone. Looks like I need to start calling first."

"That's generally a good idea." He walked to her car with her.

"I'm sorry for how I treated you, Mitch," she said abruptly, seriously. "I've regretted it for years. I was so immature."

He hadn't realized how much he'd needed to hear that from her. It opened up a place in his heart he'd kept closed and locked. "Bygones, Mar. But thank you. I could've handled things better myself then, too."

"I've been wanting to return the money I made you give me for my share of the house. Just because it was technically legally mine didn't mean I should've forced you to give it to me. The money's been in an account that I haven't touched since the first year. I'll write you a check."

"There's no need." Everyone seemed to be giving him money these days. It was a little overwhelming.

"It's necessary to my peace of mind. My husband agrees. I heard you were out of the country or I would've already repaid you."

"Are you happy? Annie told me about your kids, and that you're pregnant with twins."

"My life is great. John's a good dad and a wonderful husband." She opened her car door. "I don't know how I can talk to Annie now, at least not until the truth is out."

"I think she feels the same, but don't let all this stop you from becoming friends. We've both moved on. I'm okay with it if you are."

She hugged him. He felt the hard roundness of her belly for a few seconds. Suddenly he longed to have a child. With Annie. To watch her belly grow, to hold her hand while she was in labor, to see his child come into the world.

Fate, he thought, accepting it as he always did. Marissa had been brought here for a reason. They'd needed to forgive each other. They'd done so without saying the words, but they'd forgiven. "I'm glad you came by," he said.

"Me, too."

She drove off. He stood in the yard watching long after her car disappeared. His boots felt stuck, as if in concrete. His body had doubled in weight. He couldn't move. Everything he'd clung to for years was disintegrating, leaving his emotions naked and raw. He couldn't hate her anymore. He couldn't hate himself for how cold he'd been to her through the divorce, making life even harder for both of them. They'd both made mistakes. Big mistakes.

He'd paid way too long for his. She'd moved on with her life and was happy. Glowing, even. That was what he wanted now.

Except that now he'd gotten himself into a predicament he might not be able to extricate himself from.

Payback could be hell.

It wasn't quite dark when Annie got home. Everything was quiet, too quiet. The chickens were in the coop. The dog didn't come bounding to greet her. The yard looked orderly.

Then her front door opened and Mitch was standing there, a welcoming expression on his face. Bo shoved past him and raced to her, jumping up.

"Bo, down," Mitch said. He'd been working with him, and with Austin, to get the dog trained. He was fine with either man or boy, but he didn't take orders from her.

Yet, she thought. She'd worked with him when...

When Mitch was gone.

"You get everything done?" Mitch asked as she climbed the stairs.

"I think so. More people came to help, too. Someone will take a load of peaches to her San Francisco buyers tomorrow morning, which will ease that burden for Ginny and her husband." She hugged Mitch, then stayed in his arms, relaxing against him. "How'd things go here?"

"Would you like to see?"

"Of course."

They held hands as they walked to the barn. He turned on the lights.

"It's not finished yet, but you can see what it'll look like."

"Yes. Neat. Structured. Everything easy to find. I won't know where anything is." She grinned, pleased.

"You get to put everything away. That's the point— to be able to find what you need. I'll probably finish up while you're at the market tomorrow."

She studied his face. "Are you exhausted?"

"Not particularly. Why?"

"You seem unusually calm."

"The calm before the hurricane, maybe." He wrapped her close. "I'm anxious."

"So am I."

"Are you hungry?"

"I ate three perfectly ripe, sweet peaches. I don't need anything at the moment. Did you eat?"

"Cookies and ice cream."

"I'm thinking we might need steak to fortify ourselves for what's ahead," she said.

He nuzzled her neck. "Let's shower together first."

The phone was ringing when they got inside. It was Austin, again. "Hey, honey. How're you?"

"I miss you, Mom."

"I miss you, too." She didn't want to put words in his mouth, so she didn't ask questions, but waited for him to speak. When he didn't, she asked, "How's the weather? I hear San Diego is perfect this time of year."

"It's okay. Not hot. Dad says it's overcast in the mornings, something called a marine layer."

"Have you seen the ocean?"

"For a little bit on the drive to his place. We're supposed to go play in it, maybe tomorrow."

"That'll be fun. You haven't done that before."

"Yeah." He finally began to sound enthusiastic. "I can watch the surfers. I'll try to bring you home a shell."

"That would be great."

Her talkative boy went silent again.

"Are you tired after your long day?" she asked, aware of Mitch's interest in the conversation. He looked as if he would grab the phone himself if he could, offer his own kind of comfort and encouragement.

"I guess. Can I call you tomorrow?"

"You can call me anytime at all, honey. If I'm out in the yard and don't hear the phone ring, just leave me a message, and I'll call you right back. A day—"

"At a time," he said, finishing her sentence. "Night, Mom. I love you."

"I love you, too."

She cradled the phone gently. "I think it's not what he expected and he's disappointed. I don't know why, however."

"He's never been away from you before." Mitch rubbed her back. "Give him a day or two to adjust."

"You're right. I know you're right. I've just never heard him so down before. Angry, yes, even hurt. But not down."

"Wouldn't Rick call you if there was something seriously wrong?"

After a minute she nodded. "Yes, of course he would." She let that thought settle, then said, "I believe we have a date in the shower."

"I was here to pick you up on time, but you had all that primping to do."

She smiled, enjoying his sense of humor.

Later she decided that she was never going to get

into the shower again without thinking about this perfect night.

And no matter what happened at the end of the week, she would have no regrets.

Chapter Sixteen

"I want to come home."

It was Wednesday night, only the third full day of Austin's visit. He sounded pitiful, Annie thought, his depression having worsened daily. "Your dad will bring you home on Sunday, honey, just like we planned."

"Tonight. I want to come home tonight."

Panic set in. Annie sat on a kitchen chair. Mitch was outside rounding up the chickens. "What's going on?"

"I don't want to talk about it. I just want to come home."

"You need to tell me why, Austin."

"Just tell Dad he has to bring me."

Annie rubbed her forehead. "Let me talk to him."

"Okay."

As she waited, her mind whirled with possibilities of why he was cutting his visit short. Four days short. As a mom, she was worried. As a woman who'd been enjoying sexual freedom and satisfaction, she was annoyed.

"Hey, Annie," Rick said.

"What's going on? Why does he want to come home so soon?"

"Got me. He hasn't been happy the whole time. I've been doing my best, but he won't snap out of it."

Snap out of it? "Then I guess we need to accommodate him."

"I can't just drop everything. We have tickets for Sunday. I might be able to move them up to Saturday, except we have plans for Saturday that can't be changed. You'd have to come get him."

She needed to think it through. "Hold on a second." She rested the phone against her thigh and considered her options before she spoke again. "Could you drive him to LAX? They have a direct flight to Medford."

After a long pause, Rick said, "I can do that. It'll have to be tomorrow, not tonight."

"Of course. Will you make the arrangements?"

"Yeah. Listen, Annie, until we know what's bothering him, I can't do this again."

"Do what? See your son?" Anger swept through her in an instant.

"You know that's not what I mean."

"I don't know that, especially since you hadn't bothered to see him for a year."

"Look, you're upset right now. So am I. Let's talk about this later."

"Let me talk to Austin."

In a few seconds, Austin picked up the phone. "Mom?"

"Here's the plan." She outlined what would happen. "All right? Are you comfortable flying by yourself if you don't have to change planes?"

"Yeah."

"Okay. Your dad will let me know your schedule. I'll be there to pick you up."

"And Mitch."

Annie tried not to react to the insistence in Austin's voice. She knew he was attached, but apparently that attachment had intensified during the time spent with his father.

"I don't know what his schedule is, honey. It'll depend on when your plane lands."

"He'll change his plans for me."

All sorts of caution bells rang for Annie. "We'll see. I'll talk to you in the morning. I love you."

"Bye."

"What's going on?" Mitch came into the room.

She wondered how long he'd been there. She explained the situation.

"You don't think he's being abused, do you?" Mitch asked.

"By neglect, maybe, but not action. Physically, it's not even a remote possibility."

"Then do you really think he should get his way on this? The only way their relationship can improve is by spending time together, don't you think?" Mitch grabbed a glass from the cabinet and filled it with water. "I'm not trying to tell you how to parent. It's just an outsider's perspective. I've never been a parent, so I'm just talking off the top of my head here."

"I appreciate the input." She put her arms around him and laid her head against his back. After a minute he set down his glass and turned, wrapping her close. "I'll know how to handle it in the future once I know what's upsetting him," she said.

"I'm being selfish, too, I admit," he said. "I thought we had more time."

"You can't possibly be more disappointed than I am."

Mitch was sure that wasn't true. Sleeping next to her had been the highlight of his return to the Red Valley, hell, maybe the highlight of his entire life. He woke up frequently, assuring himself she was there, pulling her even closer, sometimes rousing her with kisses. Sometimes she roused him. If he hadn't had the dwindling supply of condoms to prove it, he wouldn't have believed he could have sex so many times in so few days. And that didn't count the times they'd been creative in ways not to need them.

He'd arranged for Buckshot and a gentle mare to be ready tomorrow afternoon for their ride. Now that would be canceled.

"I want to go pick him up by myself," Annie said, stepping back a little.

"Why?"

"Because I'd like to get to the bottom of his issues, and being in a vehicle is a good place for that. We'll have an hour to talk it out."

Mitch grabbed his empty water glass, moving out of range to refill it. "Based on what I overheard of your side of the conversation with him, he wanted me to be there."

She closed her eyes for a few seconds. "He's gotten too close to you, Mitch. You'll be leaving soon. We need to deal with that ahead of time, not just after."

She was right, absolutely, undeniably right. "Okay, I get it. I'll stay here."

Her relief was visible. "Thank you."

He didn't want their last night alone to be anything but perfect, so he proposed an idea he'd been thinking

about for a couple of days, one he'd planned for the last
night before Austin came home.

"Since we won't get to go skinny-dipping at the river
tomorrow, which I know disappoints you," he said, "I'd
like to suggest something for tonight."

"Why do I have the feeling I'm going to need con-
vincing?"

"You're a reluctant adventurer."

"What's your daring plan, cowboy?"

"After dark, I move my truck into the yard, make a
bed out of the back and we make love under the stars—"

"Okay."

"We don't have to spend the whole night, just—"

"Okay, Mitch."

"Part of— What? Did you say okay?"

"Twice." She grinned. "I've got a couple of air mattresses."

He was surprised she'd agreed so readily, but he sure
wasn't going to argue. "If you'll give me the mattresses,
I'll make up a nice bed for us."

While Annie made dinner, he fixed a cozy bed then
showered. When they were done eating, he ran a warm
bath for her. After letting her soak for a while, he washed
her back, turning the moment into a massage. The steam
made her cheeks pink. Her sighs of pleasure made him
happy.

He toweled her dry, helped her put on her robe, then
carried her from the house to the truck. As they lay side
by side, fingers entwined, watching the night sky, she
asked about the constellations. He had almost an as-
tronomer's knowledge, passed on by his grandfather,
and could have navigated himself home from anywhere.

Contentment blanketed Mitch. He'd found his North
Star, his constant.

Not long ago, that thought would've sent him running to the top of Gold Ridge Mountain. Now he accepted it. He'd fallen in love with the courageous, stubborn, hard-working, beautiful Annie Barnard.

Mitch turned on his side, propping himself on an elbow. She'd left her hair down and it framed her face like a halo, seeming to light the space when there was actually no light anywhere, no moon, no front porch beacon, just stars. It was enough. What he couldn't see, he could touch.

He kissed her, savoring her as he stroked her hair then her shoulder, her arm, her abdomen, moving the sheet down, uncovering the treasure that was Annie. Sometimes she took charge, but not this time—and he was glad. He wanted to give her another night to remember. He laid his head on her abdomen and breathed in her scent, the clear night air adding something unfamiliar but good. She ran her hands through his hair as if they had all the time in the world.

"Cowboy?" she said quietly.

"What, boss?" He could feel her laugh.

"Have you spent a lot of time under the stars?"

"A fair amount."

"My family never went camping. I never went to summer camp, either. This is a first for me."

"Are you enjoying it?" He closed his eyes as she massaged his scalp, managing to arouse and relax him at the same time.

"I'm sure it'll spoil me for going camping in sleeping bags on the ground."

"Yeah, I'm liking that less and less as I get older." He explored her with his fingers, still not in a hurry, loving the way she squirmed and moaned. "You warm enough?" he asking, blowing warm air over her.

"Hot."

He settled his mouth low on her and maneuvered himself into a better position. He knew what she liked, that she responded to light touch more than heavy, slow more than fast, and then deep. He took her almost to the point of no return a few times, then asked, "You wanna be on top?"

He had no doubt about what her answer would be. She had a fondness for that position, and he wasn't complaining about it. He liked watching her, liked being able to put his hands and mouth on her breasts. It would be the image he would carry with him the most, at least in bed. Out of bed, he loved the sight of her cooking a meal, her apron tie resting on her rear.

He was attuned enough to her that he knew exactly when she would climax, but then she stopped moving. "You're not wearing a condom," she said, her voice strained.

He'd forgotten. He'd never forgotten before, not in his entire adult life. He reached for where he'd stashed them and made quick work of it.

"That could've been disastrous," she said, repositioning herself, immediately getting caught up again.

Disastrous? Not a good thing, for sure, but disastrous? All thought scattered then as she arched her back and moved against him. He joined her in the magical, miraculous, *loving* event that lasted forever and a few seconds more....

Struggling for breath, Annie collapsed onto him. He locked his arms around her.

"I'm not going anywhere," she murmured, his intensity not easing. "This was a great idea, Mitch."

He made a vague noise of agreement.

Annie's throat started to burn, and her eyes teared

up. If only they'd had more time, maybe he would've fallen in love, too. And soon there would be no secrets between them, and who knew where that would lead? If they loved each other, it might only be a stumbling stone to their future, instead of a roadblock.

Finally he loosened his hold, letting her roll onto her side next to him but keeping her close. "Why are you so tense?" she asked. Usually after sex, he was almost boneless he was so relaxed, and playful.

He didn't say anything for what seemed like a lifetime. "I'm sorry this is going to stop."

"I'm disappointed, too. But it seems like more than that. What's going on?"

"Just that."

She didn't believe him, but she didn't want to hound him about it.

"Do you want to go back into the house?" he asked.

"Not yet. This is nice." She was starting to find it hard to stay upbeat. Was this the last night they would sleep together? It felt like it. As if the impending doom hovering over them like a little black cloud was about to break loose with torrential rains.

But not at this moment, Annie reminded herself. For the rest of the night, she would enjoy herself and him. Tomorrow would happen, no matter what.

Mitch kept himself busy the next day after Annie left for the airport. He finished the shelves in the barn. He hauled huge bags of chicken feed and dog food into their own areas. The material used to line the chickens' nesting area had its own spot.

He stood back, studying the space. Much better than when he'd arrived. She could find anything now. One more item checked off his list.

The entire property was in working order, even if a lot of it was old and outdated and held together with baling wire. He was proud of what he'd done for her, for them. Austin would understand now how important it was to keep the farm organized, to know the value of a property's inventory, and keeping it tidy and in good repair.

Mitch thought he'd passed on other useful education to the boy, too. How to fish. How to repair an old truck—or at least, how engines worked and what fit where and why. Respect for traditions was no small thing.

But maybe all that would be overshadowed by Mitch not being honest from the beginning about who he was. Although that was a lesson in itself—withholding the truth was as bad as telling a lie.

Mitch knew they were home when Bo barked happily, a sound different from when other vehicles pulled into the driveway. Mitch figured Austin would jump out of the truck, greet Bo then hug Mitch.

But he climbed down slowly, his expression somber, although he did fall onto his knees to let Bo lick his face, making him laugh.

Mitch met Annie's gaze. She shook her head and shrugged. So. Austin still wasn't talking. That worried Mitch a lot.

"Hey," Austin said, not making eye contact.

"Did you see the ocean?" Mitch asked.

"Yeah. It was big. And salty. The waves were kinda scary. Nothing like our river." He gave Mitch a quick look. "I missed you."

"I missed you, too. I had to gather eggs. Got my hand pecked a few times."

"Guess I can't ever go away again."

Mitch decided it was best not to comment on that.

Austin grabbed his suitcase from the backseat and headed to the house.

"I take it he's not talking," Mitch said to Annie.

"He said little, and none of it enlightening. I hope he opens up at some point. I don't think I can send him back to Rick for a visit without knowing what happened."

"I get that." Would the boy open up to him, instead? "How'd you spend your time?"

"Finishing up the barn. You still need to shelve some things, but the rest is done."

"I don't know how I can thank you."

"We helped each other." He wanted to pull her into his arms. Instead he folded them across his chest.

"Mom!" Austin called from the porch. "Brenna James is on the phone."

"Be right there!" Excitement radiated from her. "I've been so anxious to know what her plans are."

Mitch waited her out by checking on the new plantings in the high tunnel. Lettuce leaves were poking through the soil. She could start a new batch by the end of the week.

When she joined him in the greenhouse, she looked happy but also bewildered.

"Brenna has an idea—a charity dinner here on the farm to benefit the food bank. It'll be a big deal, a spectacular meal and entertainment, and something she'd like to make an annual event, at least." She drew a big, shaky breath. "And she's considering partnering with me here."

"Is that something you want?"

"I don't know. I need to sort it out and think it

through. For the moment, I'll focus on the event. Her idea is that we till part of the back field, lay down plywood floors and erect a big tent."

"When is this supposed to happen?"

"In a month, mid-September. It'll be the last of the summer harvest for most of us." She laid a hand on his arm. "Can you stay on until that's done?"

It would please his father, that much Mitch knew, but he was done pleasing his father. He wanted to get back to the ranch, to his own home, to whatever new working situation his father was going to grant him. Leaving Annie and Austin was going to be hard, but leaving meant he could court her properly, an optimistic goal if ever there was one.

"It would make more sense to put up a couple more high tunnels that you can use forever than to rent a tent," he said. "A month from now the weather should still let you be able to roll up the sides so that your guests can mingle between them."

"I agree it makes sense, but I can't afford them, unless I can get another grant. It took six months to get the last one."

Marissa had a check for him that would cover two high tunnels and much more. He could be an investor in the farm, too. Except he didn't think she would take money from him. Not after she found out who he was.

"Talk to Brenna and see what she says."

"I will. I'm going to meet her in town in an hour, between her lunch and dinner crowds. If you don't mind staying here with Austin?"

"Not at all."

"Thanks. You didn't answer my question about staying on," she said.

"We'll talk about it later. I can see you're anxious to go see her."

"I'm afraid to hope," she said, a little breathless. "I didn't think I'd want a partner, but the right partner, one like Brenna, with her contacts? I could have the acres behind the house productive by next year." She lifted her chin a little. "I'll show those Morgans and Ryders."

"Isn't it enough to prove it to yourself?"

A few beats passed. "Yes. Yes, it is. Thank you for reminding me of that."

She went into the house then came out soon after and drove off. Mitch waited for Austin to come to him and kept himself busy in the high tunnel until he heard the screen door slap shut.

"Whatcha doing?" Austin asked.

"Setting up the irrigation for the next batch of lettuces."

Austin drew closer to watch. Mitch showed him how to clear the lines of dirt.

"I suppose you'd like to know why I came home early," Austin said after a while.

"I'm curious." He didn't look at the boy but kept fiddling with the irrigation hose.

"He's got a new son," Austin blurted out harshly. "A whole new family."

Mitch zeroed in on him. He set down the hose and gave Austin his full attention. "What do you mean?"

"I mean he's living with a woman, Sharlene, and she has two kids, Jeremy and Rachel. He loves them more than me."

"How do you figure that?"

"He plays with them. He tickles them. He tucks them into bed."

"And he didn't do any of that with you?"

He shook his head. "They're getting married on Saturday. I was supposed to be there for it, but I couldn't. I just couldn't, you know?"

Mitch knew if anyone had sprung a surprise family and wedding on him, he would be mad and hurt, too.

"He figured I would be okay with it. He didn't even tell me on the ride to his house. We walked in and there they all were, waiting for us. I felt stupid."

Mitch set his hands on Austin's shoulders. "You are absolutely entitled to feel the way you do. He should've told you—or your mom so that she could. He's the one at fault. But, Austin, messing up that way doesn't mean he doesn't love you. Or that you've been replaced. He's one of those people who doesn't know how to share anything potentially emotional. I hope you'll be able to forgive him and continue to have a relationship with him. He'll always be your dad."

"I wish *you* were." He spoke quietly and at the ground, so that Mitch wasn't sure he'd heard him correctly.

"I wish *you* were my dad," Austin said more loudly, looking Mitch in the eye. "I told my mom to get you to fall in love with her. She says you didn't. Why not? Everyone loves her."

Mitch had never been backed into so tight a corner before. He couldn't admit to Austin that he'd fallen in love, not without telling Annie first. He couldn't get the boy's hopes up that way. "You're very special to me, Austin."

His words weren't enough to satisfy Austin, and Mitch knew it, even before Austin ran off, Bo at his heels.

The tangled web he'd created was now starting to suffocate. Tonight, without fail, no excuses, he would tell Annie the truth.

Chapter Seventeen

"I hope you're hungry," Brenna said to Annie after she arrived at the restaurant.

"I am, actually." She hadn't been able to eat, she'd been so filled with worry about Austin.

"Good." Brenna waved at a young woman working in the kitchen. "I'd like your opinion on a new dish, a cold, gingered beet salad with pistachios and deep-fried shallot rings."

The server brought the gorgeous dish and some bread. "Heaven," Annie said, savoring the creation. "You put the most interesting combinations of flavors together."

"I'm going to open a second restaurant in Redding next spring. I'm looking for a site now."

"Where will you work?"

"I'll go back and forth for a while, but once I feel comfortable with the staff I have in place there, I'll be here most of the time. This is home. I'm planning on you for certain produce. I assume you want to increase your operations so that you can make enough money to live on."

"That's my goal. It's hard to accomplish when I can only afford to do things one at a time."

"How about if that situation changed? How about if we partner up? Restaurants aren't particularly profitable ventures, either, but I'm lucky in that I'm in a position not to worry too much about money. You and I have the same worldview, I think, and I believe we can help each other. I like knowing where my food is coming from, how it's raised, how it can be picked the same day as serving it. You need steady customers you can count on. I can get you an in with a lot of other restaurant owners and probably some grocers. Your produce could be presold."

Annie set down her salad fork, having finished eating while Brenna spoke. "I'll be honest. Everything you say sounds wonderful—except I'm not sure I want a partner. I want to make it on my own. It's important to me."

"Most people get bank loans to get started. Isn't that considered making it on their own?"

"Those are loans that are paid back, not partnerships, where someone else has a piece of the action."

"I understand that." Brenna tapped her fingers on the tabletop. "Let's both think on it, then we'll discuss it another time."

"That works for me. But I'm very interested in your idea for the charity dinner."

"'From Field to Table,' I think we could call it. We'll get as much donated as possible, and sell seats at a premium. I know plenty of people who will knock on doors for donations. I think we could seat about fifty or sixty at round tables."

"If I could figure out a way to get two new high tunnels, we could use those," Annie said, testing Mitch's idea. "We could build rustic farmhouse tables and serve family style. I just need to figure out how to get the structures in time."

"Why don't you let me work on that. I've got contacts everywhere." Brenna stood. "Let's go into my office. I've been putting ideas into one folder for years now, anticipating doing this."

Annie's thoughts churned with all the work involved in getting her property ready for such an event. If Mitch could stay and till her land, at least enough of it to make space for the greenhouses, that would be good.

Plus he would need to stay on, to be there to work daily, for at least a couple of weeks. Which bought her time. Austin had asked her on the way back from the airport if Mitch had fallen in love with her. She couldn't say yes then. But maybe by the time the fund-raiser was over…?

"I guarantee my kitchen is much more organized than my office," Brenna said with a shrug. "I had the folder on my desk yesterday. Oh! I left it in the kitchen. I'll be right back."

Annie wandered around the small room, glancing at framed newspaper and magazine articles praising the restaurant, the certificates of commendation for various contributions and several photos. She moved closer to one in particular, taken under an archway—Ryder Ranch, it said in iron letters.

She spotted Jim Ryder, then his son, the lawyer Vaughn. There were a lot of them, for one family. She was trying to figure out if any of them were couples, aside from the parents, when her gaze landed on a too-familiar face. Mitch.

Mitch *Ryder*.

Annie froze. Her mind went blank. Her heart stopped beating. She made herself inhale, but it hurt her chest.

Betrayed. That was the word that landed first in her mind. Hurt. Tricked. Deceived.

Used.

She had no doubt he'd been sent either to make sure her farm didn't survive or to convince her she should sell to his family. Since he hadn't done anything to make her situation worse, she decided on the latter reason. He'd been charged with getting her to fall for him, to let him convince her to sell, that his family was more worthy than the Morgans.

Worst of all, he'd used Austin, who'd fallen in love with Mitch, too.

"Are you all right?" Brenna asked, coming up behind her.

"No, I'm—I'm sorry. I need to go home."

"All right," she said after a pause. "We can talk before or after the market, if you want."

"That's fine. That's good." She gave Brenna what she hoped passed as a smile, then left the building.

She shouldn't drive yet, that much she knew, so she started walking the downtown, sitting on a bench now and then when she became overwhelmed. How could she have been so wrong about him? Why hadn't she called his bluff and let him tell her his name? She'd fallen in love fast, and it had deepened every week, but she could've recovered easier if weeks hadn't passed— and if they hadn't made love.

But he offered to tell you and you said no.

He should've insisted.

She was right on both counts.

It was almost dark by the time she felt she could safely drive herself home.

It was going to be a very long night.

"Why isn't she home yet?" Austin asked...again.

"I don't know," Mitch answered...again. He'd wait another fifteen minutes then call Brenna James.

Just as he'd made that decision he saw headlights in the driveway.

"She's back!" Austin raced out of the house to meet her. "Where have you been?" he shouted as she climbed out of the truck.

"My meeting took longer than I anticipated. I'm sorry if I worried you."

Something was wrong. Very wrong. There was no animation in her expression, none of the happiness Mitch would've expected after her meeting.

"Are you hungry?" she asked her son.

"Mitch fixed hamburgers. He made one for you, too. It's in the fridge."

"I ate at Brenna's." She hooked an arm around his neck and pulled him close, kissing his temple. "Had dessert?"

"We were waiting for you. Mitch said you made brownies."

"I think I'll give you two some time alone," Mitch said, heading to the door, seeing she was wound tight. "I've got some work to do in the shed."

She'd found out his last name, Mitch was sure of it. It was the only explanation for her sudden change in attitude. He toyed around with his truck and straightened items in the shed until she finally came outside. An hour had passed.

She walked with purpose, and in her hand was his

duffel bag. Gut-punched, he couldn't do anything but stand there and watch—and hope she would listen to him. But as he waited, a vise squeezed his chest.

"I packed your bag, Mr. Ryder," she said, stopping at the tailgate, heaving his duffel into the truck bed. "I figure you know why."

"I would've told you tonight."

"Right."

He came up next to her. She didn't back away, but her eyes were frigid. "I tried to tell you before."

"And I didn't let you, but frankly, you should've over-ridden that, given what you knew, and how I felt about the—*your* family."

"My father didn't send me here. Everything I told you was true. I wasn't ready to go home, and my truck broke down. I ended up here, and you mistook me for someone else, and it became like a game—"

"A game?" she repeated, recoiling. "I was a *game* to you?"

Panic gripped him. "That's not what I meant. I meant the beginning was kind of like that, not for long. Just until I found out that my dad and Shep Morgan were competing to buy your property."

"Hoping I would fail."

"And I wanted you to succeed, so I figured out a way to stay and help. That's also the truth." Was he getting through to her? At least she hadn't left yet.

"We slept together," she said.

"Also honest. I wanted you from the second I met you."

Her voice went low and harsh. "My son loves you. I will never forgive you for letting that happen. After all the disappointment with his father, now this?"

"I love him, too." He tried to cup her shoulders but she jerked back. "I love you, Annie."

Her jaw dropped. "Since when?"

"Since the beginning, I think, but I knew for sure, let myself believe it, last night."

"If that's true, why didn't you tell me last night?"

"Because I needed to reveal my identity first. And because if you didn't love me back, I didn't want to lose out on what could be our last time together."

She threw her arms open. "How am I supposed to trust you now?"

"You can believe in what we've accomplished together and what we've shared. Believe that making love truly was that for me. I would've forgotten to wear a condom last night if you hadn't said anything. I never forget that." She'd said it would've been disastrous. That had hurt. "I didn't care if you got pregnant. It would've only sped up the process for me. Please believe me."

She shook her head again and again. "I don't know what to believe. Most of all, I don't want Austin to get hurt, and I don't see that it's possible. I can't look at you without feeling used."

"Used?" It was a hard, ugly word. "Never, Annie. Never. I had no agenda except to help you keep your farm, to take some of your load off, and to make you happy. I don't want him hurt, either. He confided in me what went wrong at his dad's house. I've encouraged him to tell you. I think he will."

"You see? You've even usurped my role as parent."

"Annie," he said quietly, "if I'm gone when he wakes up, he's going to be upset, I have no doubt. But he'll recover from that. If you were gone...I can't even put it into words. It's easy for him to talk to me because we're not related. It doesn't mean he loves me more. He doesn't."

"He barely spoke to me on the drive home."

"It had nothing to do with you. He'll tell you." His throat was on fire. His heart was breaking into a thousand pieces. Regrets tumbled through him, fast and furious. He admired her stubbornness—it was what would make her succeed in the end. But it also meant she wouldn't back down from sending him on his way. He'd hurt her too much. He'd hurt her son. He might be able to get past the first charge, but not the second.

"This is too painful," she said, backing up. "Please go."

"What will you tell Austin?"

"That your family needed you."

He memorized her face, wished he could wipe out the hurt in her eyes and the fierce pain inside himself. "I love you, Annie Barnard. You're the best woman I've ever known. You didn't deserve this, and I'm sorry."

He touched a finger to his hat then walked past her and climbed into his truck. She headed across the yard and was in the house before he'd finished backing out.

He'd been devastated when his grandfather died, but death was part of life, expected, even as it was mourned. *This,* this loss of the woman he loved, wasn't expected or usual or easily recovered from. He remembered with clarity when Austin confided that she cried sometimes at night when she thought Austin couldn't hear her. Would she cry now? Or was she too angry for that? Too heartsick?

Mitch drove down her driveway for the last time, navigated the twenty miles to Ryder Ranch and pulled up in front of his own house, where the lights were on.

He would have no privacy with Adam and Brody there, but he had nowhere else to go.

His brothers were watching an old John Wayne movie. Usually he would've plopped himself in front of the TV with them. Not this time.

"Don't ask," he said as he walked through the living room. "My bed's free, I hope."

"Yes," Adam said. "We cleaned up the bathroom, too. All yours."

"Thanks. I'll see you in the morning."

He heard them go to bed an hour later. Even if they heard him get up, they would stay in their rooms. He wandered through the living room, dining room and kitchen, seeking a sense of home, not finding it. It wasn't because he'd been gone so long but because of who wasn't there. Annie and Austin were what made a home for him, no matter if they were in a tent or a castle.

He went outside and sat on a porch step, leaned his back against a post. He was thirty-six years old and what had he accomplished? Got married and divorced in the same year. Was a cattleman without cattle of his own. Had coped so poorly with his grandfather's death, he'd run away rather than face it.

And now he'd hurt not just Annie but Austin.

He had to make it right.

Annie had read once that the sense of being abandoned was one you carried your whole life, that the fear of it never went away. She believed it. Worse, Austin was going to get mired in it, too.

She sat on her front porch after Mitch left, a blanket wrapped around her, with a clear view of the empty shed.

I love you, Annie Barnard. His words haunted her.

They'd both made mistakes in this relationship, and maybe she could've gotten past his if he'd included marriage in his confession. He hadn't. Love, but not marriage.

She'd believed she wouldn't ever want to marry again, but he'd made a liar out of her. She'd fallen in love with him, wanted to marry him, have his children.

But he hadn't brought it up, and now she had to face Austin in the morning and tell him Mitch was gone.

Annie's throat closed at the thought. Tears burned her eyes then started to spill. She'd tried so hard to shield her son from pain after being treated so casually by his father, and she felt she'd been mostly successful with that. But Mitch was different. Mitch had paid more attention to him from the beginning, patiently mentoring him, teaching, advising. Caring.

She swallowed hard around the lump in her throat. She didn't want to cry, didn't want him to be worth her tears. But the tears came anyway, for a long time and with passion. She banged her fists on the armrests of the rocker, pressed her hands to her eyes to stanch the avalanche of tears that wouldn't stop and wondered if her life would ever be the same.

She was still in the rocking chair on the porch when Austin came looking for her as the sun rose.

He knelt in front of her. "Where's Mitch?"

"He's gone."

"Gone where?"

"His family needed him. He went to help." She must look a wreck, as if she'd been crying all night. Austin didn't call her on it.

"When will he be back?"

"I don't know, honey. Maybe not ever."

"Mitch wouldn't do that," he said with unconcealed anger. "He wouldn't go without saying goodbye."

"He had to leave last night."

"You made him go, didn't you?" Austin stood on shaking legs. "You said he couldn't stay here any more. I *hate* you."

He raced into the house. She'd known it wouldn't be easy. She hadn't known it would be devastating.

Things got better day by day. Annie and Austin were used to it being just them, and they slipped back into their old routine, more somber, less cheerful, but coping and recovering.

Then it was the first day of school. At the end of the driveway, Annie waved goodbye to Austin when the bus picked him up, and she was faced with being alone all day, five days a week.

She'd barely reached her yard when a vehicle pulled in. Only one person she knew had a five-window truck, and here he was.

She didn't know whether to kiss him or punch him out.

Chapter Eighteen

"What now?" Annie asked. "Were you lying in wait? You think I'll sleep with you because Austin is gone?"

Mitch was so happy to see her he almost couldn't speak. "That's not why I'm here. Although I wouldn't say no if you offered it."

Indignant, she opened her mouth. He cut her off. "Everything said between us has to be the truth now. I'm only telling you the truth, Annie. I'm here to help you get ready for the food bank event. I'll till your land and do whatever else you need."

"Why?"

"Because I owe you. And because I love you." He saw her react to that, not in disbelief exactly but maybe in shock that he would say it. "Feel free to be honest in return."

"I honestly don't need to tell you anything."

He smiled a little grimly, knowing he deserved what-

ever punishment she doled out. "I've really missed you."
He held up a hand. "I'll show up every day right after
the bus picks up Austin, and I'll leave before he gets
home. He'll never know."

She had that look on her face that told him she was
torn between sending him hiking or accepting his help.

"How is Austin?" he asked, needing to know where
things stood there, too.

"Hurt at the beginning, but then when I told him
you were one of the Ryders, it helped start his healing."

He must've winced, because she added, "Honesty,
you said."

"Even if it hurts. What's happening with the high tunnels? Are you going to have to put up a tent, after all?"

"Brenna's working on it." She rubbed her forehead. "I
admit I've been feeling overwhelmed with what needs
to be done. I just don't want to get close to you again."

A ray of hope pierced his heart and warmed him.
He didn't care if he started the reconciliation with baby
steps, as long as it started. "We don't have to talk except
for you to tell me what needs to be done."

The sound she made combined laughter and frustration. "Austin's been learning to till with the tractor.
Since I don't need straight planting lines where I'll be
putting the high tunnels or the tent, I've just let him have
fun with it. It's messy."

"I don't want to take a job away from him. How
would you explain that?"

"Believe me, he's regretted being taught how to drive.
He's not really ready for that responsibility. I can tell
him I got help. That's all he needs to know. It has to
be finished soon so it can sit for a couple of weeks. It
needs to settle."

"Then I'll get right to it. Is it staked off?"

She nodded.

He started to turn away. She almost touched his arm, but pulled back her hand before she did. "I thought you were going to help your family with the haying."

"I did that all last week. There's more, but they can manage without me."

A vehicle turned into her driveway. Once again Marissa had dropped by without calling first. She poked her head out the window.

"Sorry! I figured you'd be alone, Annie. I thought we could celebrate the first day of school. I brought scones! Should I go?"

"No," Mitch and Annie said at the same time, but didn't smile about it.

"I'll get to work on the field. You enjoy your visit," Mitch said, sauntering away. "Morning, Marissa."

"How're you doing, Mitch?"

"I've been better," he called over his shoulder.

Marissa eyed Annie. "Trouble in paradise?"

"Want some tea?"

"Ah. None of my business. Okay. Sure, tea would be great."

They went inside. Annie put the kettle on and tracked down some tea bags. Because the field was in sight from the kitchen window, they both gravitated there and watched Mitch work.

"I hope you're getting more than field work out of him," Marissa said. "You could use a little unwinding."

Annie couldn't help it. She laughed. "That may be true, but that's not part of his job description." And she missed it a whole lot.

"You're single. He's single. Why not?"

"It's complicated."

Marissa laid a hand on her arm. "I don't know what

happened, obviously, but you know, men are just boys sometimes. They say and do stupid things. Then we do stupid things in return. But I can tell you this—he's a really good guy, Annie."

Annie said nothing. How could she? She knew more than Marissa did. "Is this weird, us being friends?" Annie asked.

"Probably. Who cares? But as your friend I can say that if I were single and had a sexy man getting all sweaty and manly in my back forty, I'd be all over him."

After that they talked about everything except Mitch. By the time Mitch took off before Austin's bus arrived, Annie had been down memory lane in her head several times of their few nights together. He said he would show up every day. Could she survive that? Could she resist him?

She was so afraid she would invite him back into her bed, which would solve nothing.

Well, not nothing.

Over time, Annie learned she was resistant and he was persistent. They established a routine that continued for weeks. At first they barely spoke, but eventually she invited him inside for lunch, where it was hard to avoid conversation.

Mitch was finally free to tell her about his past, the good and the bad, and was glad and relieved to do so. In turn, she doled out personal information in tiny bits that he was able to sew together into a quilt of her life—parents who loved her but were irresponsible, a hunger for friends that was never satisfied because they moved so often, a marriage of two people in need of partners but without the depth of love that sustained the best relationships through the harsh realities of life.

He told her about Marissa's visit and that they'd forgiven each other, that he'd finally laid his grandfather to rest in every sense of the word. And that he'd forgiven himself for encouraging his grandfather to go through a course of chemo when he hadn't wanted to. He'd done it for Mitch, but it hadn't helped, had only stalled the inevitable and added a great deal of pain to his grandfather's life.

The day he shared that sorrow with her, she hugged him. They were interrupted by a phone call. He never knew what would've happened otherwise. At the end of that day, as he did the end of every day, he told her he loved her right before he got into his truck and drove away.

Mitch was stuck between the proverbial rock and a hard place. He wanted to ask Annie to marry him, but he had to know Austin would be okay with it. If he spoke to Austin first, he could either turn his back on Mitch and destroy his chances to make things permanent or Austin could be excited and anxious, and then be disappointed if Annie said no. Annie would never forgive him for that.

Austin didn't know his mother and Mitch had been spending hours together, five days a week. Didn't know Mitch loved her so much he would do anything for her, even climb up on the barn roof. Mitch believed that he'd slowly and steadily removed barriers between them, but Austin was the final one, and it was a big one.

Ten days before the event, Mitch arrived and found Annie sitting on the porch steps, elbows on her thighs, chin in her hands. Bo sat right next to her, nudging her, as if in sympathy.

Mitch joined her on the stairs. "What's going on?"

"Brenna just called. The agency rejected my grant for the high tunnels. They want to see how I do with this first one. Good thing we'd already reserved a tent. And it's not even going to cut into the profits, because Marissa and her husband are donating the rental fee." She sighed. "We would have so much more impact with the high tunnels. Tents don't suit farms, but I don't see any other solution."

"I could buy the greenhouses," he said.

Annie sat up straight, stunned, then finally found her voice. "No."

"Why not?"

"Because I don't want to be beholden to you." Just when she'd finally relaxed around him again, he did this. He knew she wouldn't accept charity from him. Why had he offered?

"You could pay me back when you can."

She studied his face. She'd been doing that a lot lately, getting to know him in a way she hadn't before, up close and personal. He'd opened up, showed her his vulnerabilities. Every day he told her he loved her. Every single day. She'd been waiting for the time when he stopped saying it, for when he got tired of waiting to hear the words back. She couldn't. Austin—

"Look, Annie," he said, breaking into her thoughts. "I told you Marissa paid me back. I've got enough without it. It would make me happy if you would use it."

"No. Thank you." Although it was tempting. "I don't have a clue when I could pay you back. Once I've proven myself, I can reapply and get grants for at least one more high tunnel."

"You know, I have a lot invested in this place, too. I stood up to my father. More than anything, I want you to succeed. Why are you fighting taking a little help? It makes no business sense. Anyone would tell you that."

She saw his frustration growing. "I appreciate the offer. I do."

"But…" he said, providing the answer himself.

She watched him stare into space, then walk over to his truck and climb inside. Panic set in. He'd reached his breaking point. He was going to walk out of her life and not come back. He'd had enough of her resistance. He would give up, find another woman, get married, have babies with her. Grow old together. Bounce grandchildren on his—

No. He couldn't do that. The mere thought of it felt like a knife in her heart.

Annie had started to stand, to call out to him, when he slammed the door shut and came back, stirring up dust, reminding her of how he'd looked that first day coming up her driveway. In fact, he was wearing the same clothes today, same boots, same belt buckle, even. He'd looked sexy then, and he still did now. But she knew what kind of man he was down deep now, and that made him the sexiest man alive.

"There's another option," he said, sitting next to her again, but closer. "I was saving it for a better time, the perfect moment, but sometimes life is too messy for perfection."

He took her hand, not letting go when she tried to pull back, afraid of what he was about to say.

With his other hand, he flipped open a small, square box, revealing a white gold band with a single round diamond. It was perfect. He understood her. She wouldn't have wanted lots of glitter or flash.

"I love you with all my heart," he said, a deep, abiding tenderness in his eyes. "I want to be your partner in everything, this farm, my house, my family's ranch, parenting. Life. I'm asking you to marry me, Annie Bar-

nard. I want you by my side for the rest of our lives."
He smiled a little. "Your wedding gift will be two high
tunnel greenhouses. I'll bet not many women get offered that."

She tried to hold back the tears, but they spilled out
anyway.

"Is that a yes?"

"I can't," she whispered, closing the lid on the beautiful ring and everything it represented.

"Why not?"

"Because Austin's decided to hate you."

The school bus stopped at the end of the driveway.
Austin waved then jogged up the road—until he spotted Mitch waiting for him on the porch. Then Austin
stopped, ignoring Bo jumping around him.

"Where's my mom?" he asked.

"Inside. She's letting me talk to you alone. I'd appreciate a few minutes, Austin." Mitch had been scared a
few times in his life, but it was always for his physical well-being, not anything like this. His entire future
rested on his saying the right thing to this boy.

"You left. You never even said goodbye. Why should
I talk to you?"

"I'm hoping the fact I love you and I love your mother
will be enough for you to listen. Just listen. Or ask questions. Whatever you feel like doing."

Apparently those words weren't the right ones, because he looked away. Mitch waited, still scared.

"Okay," Austin said, sitting on the porch steps, far
to one side.

Mitch sat, too, on the opposite side, giving the boy
space.

"First," Mitch said, "I'm sorry I left without telling

you goodbye. Things got…difficult between your mom and me, and I had to go. But I came back the first day of school, and I've been here while you've been in class ever since, trying to make things up to your mom, trying to win her back."

"Win her back? You mean there *was* something going on before?"

"Yes. You know I didn't tell her or you my last name. Here's why." Mitch phrased the explanation as simply and succinctly as possible. "It was the wrong thing to do. I know that now. Sometimes adults make mistakes, some of 'em bigger than others. This one was major. I'm asking for your forgiveness, Austin. I want to ask your mom to marry me and for us to be a family, but I can't do it without you forgiving me."

"What if I don't?"

"I'm not leaving, if that's what you're thinking. I'll be here every day, loving you both every day."

"Even if I keep saying no, that you can't marry my mom?"

"I'll still be here. But see, the thing is, I'd like to have some kids with your mom, give you brothers and sisters, like I have. I can't wait twenty years to do that."

"You'd come every day for twenty years just to prove you'd stay?"

"A hundred years."

Austin looked away. "You're the one who's been tilling the land, getting it ready."

"Yes."

He gave Mitch a look. "Thanks."

Mitch laughed.

"If I say yes, you can marry us, where would we live?"

"We'd have to work that out. I've got a house on the

ranch, so that's a possibility. Staying on here's a possibility. There's only twenty miles separating the two places. We could modernize this one some. Make it easier on your mom with some new appliances and stuff. I promise you'll be part of the decision." Mitch eased a hand onto Austin's shoulder. "I've come to love you as if you were my blood. You'll always have your dad, and I know he loves you and will always be your dad. But I'd be here every day for you. You can count on me. I'll protect you with everything I have."

Austin swallowed hard. "My mom's been pretty sad since you left."

"Me, too. And I missed you a whole lot. I love you, bud."

"I love you, too." Austin threw himself at Mitch, his body shaking, a few sobs escaping. "I thought I'd never see you again."

"I'll be here until the day I die, loving you, loving your mom."

"Mom!" Austin hollered toward the house. "I know you're listening. Get out here."

Annie stepped onto the porch, wiping away tears. Mitch and Austin met her for a group hug. Over Austin's head, Mitch kissed her. He'd waited so long to do that.

Then he got down on one knee, opened the small velvet box again and said, "Will you do me the honor of being my wife?"

"I will. I definitely will. I love you, Mitch Ryder."

Mitch slid the ring on her finger, then he pulled something else from his pocket and handed it to Austin. "This bolo tie belonged to my granddad, and now it belongs to you. It ties us together, three generations. I'll tell you lots of stories about him, and I hope you'll wear that proudly."

Austin's eyes shimmered as he looked at his mother then slipped the bolo over his neck. "How's it look?"

Annie grasped the polished rock and slid it up a little. "I've never seen a T-shirt look so sharp."

They stood there grinning until Bo hopped up, insinuating himself into the newly formed family.

They'd found home together.

* * * * *

A sneaky peek at next month…

Cherish

ROMANCE TO MELT THE HEART EVERY TIME

My wish list for next month's titles…

In stores from 19th July 2013:

❑ How to Melt a Frozen Heart — Cara Colter

& A Weaver Vow — Allison Leigh

❑ The Cattleman's Ready-Made Family — Michelle Douglas

& Rancher to the Rescue — Jennifer Faye

In stores from 2nd August 2013:

❑ The Maverick's Summer Love — Christyne Butler

& His Long-Lost Family — Brenda Harlen

❑ A Cowboy To Come Home To — Donna Alward

& The Doctor's Dating Bargain — Teresa Southwick

Available at WHSmith, Tesco, Asda, Eason, Amazon and Apple

Just can't wait?

Special Offers

very month we put together collections and
onger reads written by your favourite authors.

Here are some of next month's highlights—
nd don't miss our fabulous discount online!

n sale 2nd August

On sale 2nd August

On sale 19th July

 # Save 20%
on all Special Releases